The

Unusual Suspects

Dominic Carrillo

CIELA/CSP Publishing

CIELA
& CreateSpace Publishing

Copyright © 2018 Dominic Carrillo
All rights reserved.
ISBN: 1548972207
ISBN-13: 978-1548972202

Editor: Jennifer Silva-Redmond

Cover design: Meira Gottlieb, Vera Prokopieva (back cover image) and Patricia Ellson (concept)

Praise for *The Unusual Suspects*:

"There's rarely a dull moment; there's juicy suspense in every subplot and plenty of close calls... (An) adventure story that celebrates the value of literature and unlikely friendship."

-Kirkus Reviews

"One of the best things I have read in awhile in coming-of-age literature. It isn't just great, it is sweet like honey."

-ReadersFavorite.com

"What a wild ride! *The Unusual Suspects* is a story about finding yourself and true friendships in the most unlikely places."

-Margie's Must Reads

"A highly entertaining and deeply profound YA novel... a heartwarming story about an unforgettable friendship."

-Candi Sary, author *of Black Crow, White Lie*

"I thoroughly enjoyed *The Unusual Suspects*... I could not put it down!"

-John Kurtenbach, *librarian*

"Readers of all ages will be captivated by the exploits of Carrillo's unusual suspects. "

-Amy Mortenson, *middle school teacher*

Dedicated to my wife, Bozhana.

ACKNOWLEDGEMENTS

Thanks to my mom and dad, Rollie and Tania, and all of my extended family. Your love and support from the very beginning has been invaluable. Thanks to my middle school students who never fail to inspire me. Special thanks to two former students—Silvia Damyanova and Sammy Underwood—who offered great feedback and crucial teenage insight. Thanks to Tricia Quinn, a trusted first reader, and to Azul Terronez for his insightful coaching. An enormous thanks to Jennifer Silva-Redmond, whose professional editing and wisdom carried me through the writing process again. My appreciation, love and respect to Bozhana, who has made key suggestions and spent many lonely nights while I typed away, consumed by a story that I hope readers will connect to.

"I regret having... said what I did to you,"
he remarked.

"Why is that?" Dantes asked.

"Because I have insinuated a feeling into
your heart that was not previously there:
the desire for revenge."

    -Alexander Dumas,
    The Count of Monte Cristo

PART I: Escape from Sofia

NIA

When that man entered my cabin, I didn't guess what he was—I mean, he didn't look half as gross as the guys back at the train station in Belgrade. I wasn't suspicious until I noticed him staring at my legs. The creep smiled at me but didn't say a word. After a few moments of awkward silence, he leapt across the aisle and pinned me down.

It was unreal how fast it happened. I wanted to yell "I'm only fourteen!" But I couldn't. He covered my mouth with one of his hairy hands and pinned my arm across my body. His face pressed against my face, he said something foreign that reeked of cigarettes and garlic. *Repulsive.* That's when I started kicking like crazy and one of my kicks got him where it counted. He grunted and pulled his hand away from my mouth for a second. I screamed and his hands went straight for my throat. I squirmed and fought, but he was way too strong. When he let go, I gasped for air before he placed his right hand over my mouth again, using his left to unbutton my jeans. I remember the thick ring on his finger was wedged under my nostril and I gagged at the smell of sweat and urine.

That's when I knew he was going to rape me.

KURT

It was only moments after I had found a semi-comfortable position that I heard a horrible, piercing scream and then a muffled, barely audible cry. It was coming from the cabin right next to mine.

If that scream had been the least bit playful, I would have let it go and tried my best to sleep until we reached Budapest at dawn. But the sound was a desperate, terrified plea for help. So I stood up and grabbed my cane as quickly as I could—which, to a young observer, would have looked pretty damn sluggish. Usually, I don't like using my cane because it makes me feel ancient. Of course, I am, but that's not the point. Depending on the time of day, I can feel anywhere between 50 and 150 years old.

On this particular occasion, I was feeling both very old and very glad I owned a cane—and not just any cane. I gripped my Royal Cane Company steel-handled mahogany rod like it was a police baton and tottered a few steps to the cabin next door.

Under normal circumstances I would have knocked, but I didn't even consider it since I could hear clear sounds of struggle inside. I opened the door and was shocked to see a stocky man with dark hair on top of a young girl. They were both fully clothed, though her pants were unbuttoned. It looked like the man was trying to take her jeans off when I interrupted them. He turned his thick head toward me with bulging, guilty eyes but he didn't make a move—apparently he wasn't threatened by an old fart like me. Maybe that's why he removed his hand from her mouth and turned back as if to cue her not to make another sound. I made eye contact with the youngster who looked terrified enough to justify my next move. I swung my mighty cane, handle forward, right at the man's shoulder. My intention was to hurt him, so he knew I meant business. But he turned his head back toward me just then, so that the side of his face met my stainless steel handle dead on. The man's eyes rolled to the back of his head and he fell to the ground like a sack of potatoes. I knelt to determine what was by then pretty obvious. I'd knocked him out cold.

What were the odds of that?

The young girl had already buttoned up her pants and was staring at me, wide eyed, without saying a word. She must have been in shock. First she was nearly raped and now the assailant lay unconscious at her feet. Petrified, she stared at me—an unfamiliar old geezer.

"Are you okay?" I asked.

She nodded at first, then shook her head, glaring at the lump lying on the floor.

"Is he dead?" she asked, without the slightest accent.

"Probably not," I said.

Frankly, he'd gotten what he deserved. I figured if he was dead they might put me in prison, but did they put 89-year-old guys in prison these days? I didn't know and didn't care to find out first-hand, so I reached my arm out to the shell-shocked girl and said the only thing that made sense:

"What's your name?"

"Nia," she said, her eyes still locked on the prone body.

"We should go."

NIA

In a kind, gentle, American voice, he asked if I was okay. What could I say?

I was far from okay. I was—I didn't know what I was. It was like I'd woken up from a nightmare, but was still dreaming.

Normally, I wouldn't have listened to the instructions of an old man in an old suit on a train from Belgrade to Budapest, but I had just been assaulted by a violent pervert, now lifeless on the ground. A red, golf ball-sized welt had already begun forming on his temple. Did I feel bad for him? Not really.

Looking away from his swelling wound, I grabbed my backpack and my book, stepped over the body, and followed the old man down the hall to the next train car.

As we walked, I asked him who he was and he said, 'I'm Kurt.'

I thought he might be joking because he hadn't said much to me, and it was kind of awkward, and then he was like, 'I'm *curt*.' Get it?

"Kurt Chavez," he added with a smile.

He didn't seem like a bad guy and he wasn't threatening at all. In fact, he looked so old I thought he might keel over and die at any moment.

KURT

Nia and I sat down in the empty train cabin facing each other. I looked at her and she gazed at her knees silently. The heavy steel wheels of the train made that familiar, rhythmic clicking noise along the track. She was taking deep breaths as if she were absorbing her recent trauma by the lungful. At first I took her for about eighteen, but now she looked more like sixteen, younger than my great-grandkid—a baby for godsakes! That scumbag had the urge to force himself on an innocent child.

I had been disappointed with the world countless times in my life. Here was yet one more reason to despair. Nia and I didn't speak, so the clicking of the wheels was our only soundtrack.

I wanted to talk to Nia, but the girl was clearly shaken up beyond words. So instead of forcing small talk, I stared out the window, pretending I could see something out in the darkness. I was close to dozing off when I heard Nia's voice crack. I looked at her and she was still avoiding eye contact. Her mouth opened and she attempted to say something but started crying instead. It was a controlled, quiet cry—tears, sniffles and some irregular noises, but nothing hysterical.

I felt sorry for the kid.

"Nia, I know you're not okay," I said, "So I'm not going to ask you again if you are. But, that man in there, did he hit you?"

"No," she said.

"What did he—

"He choked me, that's all."

"He didn't—

"No." she said, "He was trying to—

Her voice hit a brick wall. She cried some more, this time with less control.

Nia didn't say the word "rape" but I got the gist.

Even though I was about as experienced in life as you could get on this planet, I didn't know what to say. I didn't want to hug her, or even pat her on the shoulder. I wasn't her grandfather. I was a stranger. I had nothing good to say, but I had to say something.

"I'm sorry," I said.

Her whimpering slowed down and eventually became silence. The clicking of the tracks was once again the lone sound in our cabin.

NIA

It was too difficult to talk to Kurt, so I played the entire day back in my mind as if I were telling him. I had to in order to make sense of anything... It was all too much to process.

I'd packed my school backpack early that morning, except I didn't put my textbooks in it. I packed for travel. My plan was to get from Sofia to Berlin to reverse The Epic Devastation. Yeah, it was ambitious and a bit wild, but I had to do it. I put on my favorite black leather jacket, my Clash T-shirt, and some ripped jeans. I filled my bag with a few changes of clothes, two Coke Zeros, my make-up and toiletries, *The Count of Monte Cristo*, my passport, and 500 euros I'd stolen from my dad the night before.

I didn't have to worry about talking to my dad that morning because I always left for school before he got up. *Was he in his room getting ready for work, or still sleeping—hung over or just too lazy to get up and join me for breakfast?* In that particular moment, I hoped he wouldn't unexpectedly wake up while I was eating my corn flakes. I didn't want to see him. It might make my escape plan more complicated.

As usual, I ate my cereal alone at the cold granite kitchen counter.

I imagined my friends' families running around their cozy houses, getting ready for work and school, chatting, bumping into one another—the family dog wagging its tail by the door. But not in my home—no, it wasn't a home. It was my Bulgarian dad's luxury penthouse apartment in downtown Sofia. His modern, sterilized bachelor pad was exactly one kilometer from my American mom's slightly-more-comfy upscale apartment.

Though they'd been divorced for over a year, I still hadn't gotten used to flip-flopping between my busy parents each week. And I was convinced that they'd never even become accustomed to *being parents* in the first place. Some days, it seemed like they forgot I even existed. How else could they have *both* missed my fourteenth birthday party? Sure, my mom had her assistant organize it all, and my dad hired a videographer to record the whole thing, but they didn't even show up! (This was bad, but it wasn't The Epic Devastation. I will get to *that* later on.)

At 7:45 am, I checked myself in the entry hall mirror like it was just another normal school day. I judged my make-up with a nod—enough to look older than my age, but not so much that I looked trashy. I adjusted my jacket and walked out the front door without a word, a hug, or a smile.

Rounding the corner where my private school bus usually picked me and the other downtown students up, I barely broke stride as I handed Peter Petrov (fellow eighth grader) an envelope and a twenty leva bill. This was his payoff for telling the bus monitor that I was sick. The note was forged by me. The letterhead and envelope from my dad's company made it look official.

"What if they ask questions?" Peter said.

"Just tell them my nanny gave it to you," I said, "Thanks."

The note in Peter's hand said that my parents excused my absence because I had a doctor's appointment that day. The note also specified that the bus monitor was to give it to the receptionist at school. This would cover me until that evening when I was supposed to go to my mom's place. I knew it would work because my parents—who didn't speak to each other—would assume that I was attending classes all day at my posh American international school.

After I made the hand off to Peter, I continued walking toward the taxi stands on Levski Blvd. I got into the back of a cab and directed the driver to the central train station. Like most taxis in Bulgaria, the ride was smoky, fast, and quiet—aside from "Is this Love?" by Whitesnake on the radio (which, of course, cheesy as it may be, made me think about Alex and The Epic Devastation).

I paid cash at the post-Communist ticket office and the lady with rotten teeth behind the counter asked no questions as she slid me a one-way ticket to Belgrade. I guess the more-makeup-thing had worked. At my school, the foreign international students always said that the Bulgarian girls looked and acted older than their age. And they were kind of right. I was only half Bulgarian, but I probably fell into that category: a middle schooler who looked like she was in high school.

It was strange taking a seat by myself on such a grimy train. The rail car was mostly empty, which made sense. *Who needed to get from Sofia to the Serbian border on a Thursday morning at eight?* The seats were faded blue, cheap and dated. Like many aspects of life in Bulgaria, the lack of train quality reminded me that my country had been the doormat of history. When I sat down in my unwelcoming seat it hit me that, though I'd been on trains before, I'd never ridden one in my own country. The empty car also reminded me that I was going to be alone for two whole days—that is, if all went according to plan:

—*Get to Belgrade, take another train to Budapest, then on to Berlin.*

—*Check into the Berlin Radisson by Saturday afternoon.*

—*Reverse The Epic Devastation with Alex and Victoria in epic fashion!*

I'll admit to not having worked out the details yet, but I figured I'd have enough time on the train to do this. I also had my inspiration by my side: *The Count of Monte Cristo*. I hadn't finished my new favorite book yet, but brought it along to do just that. When the train started moving my stomach dropped, the reality hitting me.

—*I'm running away from my parents.*

—*I stole from my dad, ditched school, and forged documents.*

—*I'm about to illegally cross an international border.*

—*I might be way too young to pull this thing off.*

I opened my book and flipped back to one of the sections I'd highlighted for moments like these. Page 88. Faria, the old man in prison, tells Edmund Dantes:

> "*Misfortune is needed to plumb certain mysterious depths in the understanding of men; pressure is needed to explode the charge. My captivity concentrated all my*

faculties on a single point. They had previously been dispersed, now they clashed in a narrow space; and, as you know, the clash of clouds produces electricity, electricity produces lightning and lightning gives light."

I may not have understood every word exactly, but I liked it because Dumas reminded me why I needed to act: I had been wronged. I had been served "misfortune." I needed to go out into the world, take it by surprise, and confront the problem: Victoria and Alex—the cute, stupid boy I still loved. I hoped that the electricity of seeing him face-to-face would give me and him some "light."

The clicking of the railroad tracks came to my attention. It sounded like a different century. I stared at the coffee stain on the seat next to me, hoping it was coffee and not something more disgusting. That's when my phone chimed and startled me. Fear shot through me. *I couldn't get caught. Not this soon. I wouldn't let it happen. I wanted—needed—to get to Berlin.* I pulled my iPhone out of my bag and saw Anna's name across the screen. *Thank God.* She was my best friend. Maybe my only real friend. She texted:

ANNA: hey, i'm in period 1. Mr conrad... DID U ACTUALLY DO IT?!?!?!?

NIA: yeah!!! i'm on the train :D it's kinda weird but also pretty exciting

ANNA: ahahahhaha wtf!!! U r crazy, but i understand why u have to.... kinda like silvia needs to stop wearing the same yoga pants everyday!!!:D:D

NIA: haha, yeah i get what you mean. Although i'm not feeling crazy. Im sooo glad i'm not in class today

ANNA: badass!!!

NIA: ok, but seriously don't forget that you CAN'T tell anyone what i'm doing. If someone asks, tell them i'm sick. And don't post anything anywhere pls. No posts... promise..?

ANNA: i know, i know. i've got your back, nia.... But what are u gonna do??

NIA: what do u mean???

ANNA: i mean when you get to berlin????

NIA: I'm gonna surprise Alex and Vict-whore-ia and... make them feel whore-ible... then Alex will... I don't know... apologize?? Dump her and... pick me ig??

ANNA: hmmmmm....that's a lot... whatever. ur amazing and super-smart! if anyone can pull this off, you can... Vict-whore-ia is in for a shocker ;))

NIA: haha... thanks :D

ANNA: what about your parents??!?!?!

NIA: honestly they probably won't even notice i'm gone tbh, no joke.

ANNA: are you sure you feel safe? is there anyway I can help?

NIA: thanks, but i'm fine. I'm a bit lonely but fine. Finally gonna get the chance to finish monte cristo!

ANNA: such a dork...:D anyways gotta go, or i'm gonna get caught. Have fun tho and send updates!! ;))

NIA: actually, i'm gonna turn my phone off bc i heard that ppl can track you thru your phone... delete this convo pls!! Bye love you <3

ANNA: love u!!! <3

Confirmation: Anna was my only true friend. Maybe it was because I'd known her since I was in 2nd grade. Maybe it was because we were both half-Bulgarian and half-American. Maybe it was that we both had self-

24

absorbed, wealthy parents who paid to have us raised by nannies. Whatever it was, we could chat all day and night and never get sick of each other. I trusted her and knew that even if the teacher caught her in the middle of our texting exchange, she would stomp her phone into the ground before giving it up to Mr Conrad.

I can't say I liked her referring to me as "crazy" more than once, but I suppose she had to contrast her boring spot in the classroom with my solo travel adventure. Without delay, I switched off the Wi-Fi and turned off my phone. I stuffed it deep in my bag as if the deeper it went, the more untraceable I would be.

After our next stop, I peered around the train car and noticed only a handful of passengers. The clack-clack of the track was slow. It kind of made me want to sleep, but I was too energized and on alert to nap. I returned to my book and tried to settle down with the thought of being on my own.

Two hours later I was at the Bulgarian-Serbian border. Two officers boarded the train and checked passports. They made me nervous, but not too much. Everyone knew that Balkan border guards had stern demeanors but soft spots for fifty-euro bills. The chubby, deep-voiced Serbian border officer eyed my passport and asked where my parents were. I told him in Bulgarian—close enough to

Serbian—that my dad had gone to a different car to make some business calls and would be back soon if the officer wanted to wait.

He didn't.

Fifty euros saved!

My butt got sore sitting on that train for over four hours, coasting through Serbia, reading *The Count of Monte Cristo*, pondering The Epic Devastation, and dozing off from time to time. When I'd been planning my escape the night before, it was like my trip was gonna be this romantic, movie-like journey. Sherlock Holmes meets Jason Bourne, only I'd be the heroine. But it was turning out to be the opposite—mostly boring and lonely. It was actually more fun to plan my escape, and brought me back to one of the highlighted lines in my book:

> *"How did I escape? With difficulty. How did I plan this moment? With pleasure."*

At the stop in Nis, an old smelly lady boarded and sat next to me. She had a brown scarf over her head like a real old-school Soviet-era village *Baba*—grandma in Bulgarian. Her deep wrinkles meant she could be anywhere between sixty and ninety years old. The long whiskers on her chin distracted me from her warm smile.

"Dober dan," she said.

"Dober den."

"You are Bulgarian?" she asked.

"Yes, kind of," I said.

She laughed at either my uncertainty or the little differences between Bulgarian and Serbian words.

"Are you going to visit family?" she asked.

"No."

"Are you alone? Where are your parents?"

"I'm old enough to travel on my own," I asserted.

"Hmph. Not possible."

"You disagree?" I said.

I usually wouldn't bother to talk to a random, questioning Baba, but I had been alone for hours. Instead of taking me up on the age issue, this old lady took a long breath and squinted at my face for a few long seconds. It was awkward.

"What the hell is in your nose?" she blurted out.

"What?" I said. *In my nose? Oh, she means my nose ring.* "It's called a nose ring," I said. *Actually, it's a diamond stud.*

"Well, it looks awful," she said, as if I'd asked for her opinion. "It ruins your pretty face."

Hmmm. An insult and a compliment all in one. Leave it to a Balkan grandma to offer unsolicited judgments to complete strangers. But at least I understood these cultural quirks, unlike most of my non-Bulgarian classmates. They took such comments as rude, but I knew they were harmless. I just smiled at the Baba sitting next to me, scanning my face.

"Makes you look like some kind of punk with your dark make-up and that thing in your nose," she added.

"Okay," I said, not taking it personally.

"Okay, what?" She obviously didn't like my response.

"Okay, thanks for sharing," I said.

"What's wrong with you?" the Baba said, "Your whole generation is totally lost."

It might sound harsh, but it was typical random Baba behavior to jump from open disgust with my facial jewelry to dismissing an entire generation as worthless. Still, she was starting to annoy me. Rather than defend myself and my teenage comrades, I ignored her and reached into my bag for a Coke Zero. As soon as I opened the lid, the Baba grabbed the can.

"What the—"

"Calm down," she said, pulling her hand away from my soda. "I was only checking the temperature. It's warm, so you're good."

"Excuse me?"

"Cold drinks are bad for you, missy," Baba explained. "They will give you a horrible throat disease, you know. Very bad."

"Whatever," I said.

She shook her head and turned away, as if she were remembering a loved one who had fallen victim to the dreaded cold soda epidemic. I pictured this Baba warning kids on the street about the dangers of low soda temperature, while completely neglecting the artificial sweeteners and who-knows-what-other chemicals inside a Coke. It made me laugh, but I kept it to myself. If Anna were with me, she would have been cracking up. While I mused, Baba went back to checking me out, this time focusing on my jacket and ripped jeans.

"Why do young girls always want to grow up so fast?" she asked.

I didn't answer. I didn't think she really wanted my response anyway.

The Baba continued her lament: "So they can marry and work and bear the burdens of childbirth and parenting? Cooking and cleaning all day? To sit under the yoke of a man—the swines that can't do anything for themselves. The dirty cheaters!"

She'd obviously had some bad experiences.

"It all sounds pretty bleak if you put it that way," I said. I didn't want to directly say that *her life* sounded bleak.

The Baba sighed. "Well, life is bleak, missy... Yes, my husband left me, but I should've left him. The dirty pig!"

"Yeah, guys can be stupid sometimes," I said, and thought of Alex. His name alone gave me a shot of conflicting emotions. I wanted to give him a big slap across the face—then a long, sweet kiss.

"Sometimes?" the Baba blurted. "How about always!"

The Baba steamed like a boiling kettle. We didn't talk for a few uncomfortable minutes. I peered out the window and noticed the drab colors of the nameless Serbian town we were passing through. The grey exteriors of homes were cracked and crumbling. Three raggedy kids kicked a soccer ball down the potholed street.

"Do you have any kids?" I asked, breaking the silence.

"Yes, three. But they're all screwed up because of *him*," Baba said, suggesting that she still blamed her ex-husband for absolutely everything.

"That's too bad," I said, thinking of myself.

Am I screwed up? Is it because of one of my parents or is it both of their faults—or is it my fault? Or maybe this Baba is the one who's screwed up!

"Yes, but I try not to be bitter," she said bitterly. "I'm sorry, missy. Why are you on this train alone?"

"I'm going to meet my dad in Belgrade," I said, not looking her in the eye.

"Please, tell the truth. It does you no good to lie to me, child," she asserted. "I am a stranger to you. I'm getting off at the next stop anyways."

What!? Is she psychic? Does she have some weird Baba powers? There were many Bulgarians who believed that village Babas had the ability to prophesy—to tell the future. I definitely didn't want to tell her another lie.

"What difference does it make to you if I'm meeting my dad or if I ran away from home?"

"No difference to me," she said. "I'm just a curious old lady. Humor me."

"I ran away from home in Bulgaria," I said.
"Why?"
"I can't tell you."
"You can't tell me, or you can't tell yourself?" the Baba asked as she gripped the handle of her weathered grocery bag and stood up. Those last four words reverberated: *"You can't tell yourself?"*

I didn't know what to say.

The train slowed to a halt as a voice faintly announced the stop's odd-sounding name in Serbian. I looked at the Baba's face, again distracted by the patch of grey whiskers on her wrinkled chin.

"No answer, huh?" she said. "Well, good luck. You'll need it, missy."

31

Baba lifted her bag and hobbled away. She had a limp in her stride and appeared to be in dire need of a hip replacement she couldn't afford. I was bothered by her final words, but also felt sorry for her immobility and wondered if she'd make it to the exit doors before the train started moving again.

Alone now, the Baba's question filled me with just enough doubt to lead me right back to a section I had underlined in *Monte Cristo,* page 121:

> *"I regret having helped you in your*
> *investigation and said what I did to you,"*
> *he (Faria) remarked.*
> *"Why is that?" Dantès asked.*
> *"Because I have insinuated a feeling into*
> *your heart that was not previously there:*
> *the desire for revenge."*

Yes, revenge for The Epic Devastation.
Getting back at Victoria and Alex.
That's why I was going to Berlin.

Though I reached for my phone at least six times, I deliberately avoided using it. And, though I'd like to report otherwise, the rest of the train trip was very boring. Around six hours—yes, six long hours—later I was in the Belgrade train station. I'd already calculated that the best way to get to Berlin was to take a train to Belgrade first, then a separate one to Budapest. I didn't want to pay for a ticket all the way from Sofia to Berlin because it would make it easier to track me down. Yeah, I've seen enough movies to pay attention to these paranoid details.

The Belgrade train station was scary at night and I had to wait until 10:30 p.m. to board. I remember the yellow cracking paint on the walls, crude graffiti, litter on the ground, and dim lighting. Lots of refugees lingered near the ticket counters. I sat down in the only well-lit place—the terminal café—but there were suspicious-looking guys lurking everywhere. More than a few men stared at me like wolves eyeing a piece of fresh meat as they passed by my table near the doorway. Though my favorite jacket usually gave me a sense of toughness and independence, it wasn't working that night. I felt dirty and ashamed but didn't know exactly why—they were the ones being sketchy creeps. One slimy guy even smiled at me as he walked by, showing off that his tongue could fit through the space where his two front teeth were missing! *Gross.*

I finally boarded the train to Budapest, found an empty compartment to sit in, and hoped that nobody else—aside from a girl my age—would come in. If train officials or border guards asked about my parents, I planned on lying again. *They're in the bathroom. Dining car. They had an emergency.* Whatever I had to say. And if that didn't work, I'd try to pay them off.

The train horn blew and we pushed out of Belgrade.

Up to that point, I had been proud of my escape-artist self. I had made it to a *different country* without anyone catching me, and I was still going. But it wasn't at all like I'd pictured it. I had visualized traveling by day, not at night; not in an unlocked train cabin; not without my phone or anyone to talk to; not having departed from a station full of disgusting, creepy guys. *Are they on this train too? Will they be sitting next to me—or worse, sleeping next to me?* I was beginning to get scared.

Somehow, recounting my day's progress in my mind had helped me out. By the time I brought myself up to the present, I was ready to talk to the old man sitting across from me.

KURT

Nia finally spoke after a long, understandable silence.

"Thank you," she said.

"You're welcome," I said, happy to communicate. "But I can't imagine hearing your scream, ignoring it and then having a good night's sleep."

Nia's face dropped. "Are you trying to be funny?"

"Yes, well, no. I am just clarifying—I am no hero."

"I didn't say you were a hero. I said *thanks*."

The hint of attitude told me Nia was ready to talk, that was for damn sure. I got flashbacks to my own daughter when she'd made the shift into her teenage years. It was as if she went to sleep one night a sweet kid who always kissed me on the cheek, then woke up the next day a moody hormonal rollercoaster, distant and rude.

"I simply heard that you needed help and I reacted, that's all," I said. "I was a teacher for twenty-five years so I guess it's ingrained in me from all those recess duties."

"You were a teacher?"

"Yes."

She paused and adjusted.

"Were you fun or boring?"

"Probably a little of both," I said.

She smiled. I was glad and a bit surprised that she didn't seem too traumatized anymore.

"What do you do now?" she asked, as if now interviewing me to gauge trust.

"I'm retired," I said. "I used to write from time to time."

"You're a writer?" she said.

"Yeah, I suppose you could say that."

"Written any books?"

"Yeah. Four," I said, "—five if you count the one that only a dozen people bought."

"Were any of them famous?"

"Not really. The most popular was my last one, a book for youngsters called *The Wonderful World of Walter Whims*."

"Oh my god, I read that in 6th grade!" she blurted out.

I chuckled proudly, though I'd imagined my target audience closer to eighth or ninth grade.

"Well, did you like it?" I asked.

"Yeah," she said, "I don't remember much, but I liked how the title was *The Wonderful World of Walter Whims,* but Walter's life was one horrible, ridiculous problem after another. Nice job being ironic."

"Thank you."

"Do you still write books?"

"Nope."

"Why not?" she asked.

"I ran out of stuff to say."

"Oh," she said. "That's too bad."

Nia leaned back in the chair and seemed to relax for the first time.

"How old are you, Nia?"

"Is it important?"

"I think so," I said.

"I'm fourteen."

She's a kid!

"My God, where are your parents?" I asked—something I would have asked first if I'd known she was only fourteen.

"At home... in Bulgaria."

For Chrissakes! She was a minor, alone on an overnight train to Budapest, a near rape victim—and the attempted rapist may or may not have been unconscious in the next train car. I had so many questions to ask her, but only one came out:

"Nia, how did you manage to get on a train to Budapest alone?"

"I can't tell you," she said, "I mean, it's personal."

She crossed her arms and seemed uncomfortable again, so I didn't push the subject. It was a long train ride, and if she wanted to tell me more she would.

I don't remember what time it was—probably early in the morning. I'd dozed off for a few minutes when the impact of my bobbing chin hitting my shoulder woke me up. I had a nasty crick in my neck, in fact, my whole body was one damn big crick.

Nia sat across from me, sleeping much more comfortably. Her eyes were closed like a cherub's. Her dark brown wavy hair with a cowlick almost centered at her hairline reminded me of my wife, Maria, when she was young. I could hardly believe that Maria had been dead for twelve years now. *How had so many years passed without her?* But I always remembered my first vision of Maria and how perfect her hair looked and that little cowlick.

Maria—she was the reason I was on this train.

"Um," Nia said.

Her voice and wide eyes startled me.

"Don't tell me you're having some kind of Nabokov moment."

"Excuse me?" I said.

"You're staring at me like I'm Lolita."

"I was not," I said, offended.

"Then why were you staring?"

I paused before explaining, grieved that my wife was no longer alive and a bit annoyed at Nia's suspicions.

"I was admiring your hair because it reminded me of my wife's."

"A lot of females have brown hair, you know," she said like a smart aleck.

"True, but not everyone has a cowlick on their hairline," I noted.

"A *what*?"

"A cowlick," I said and pointed to my hairline and made a little swirly motion with my index finger.

Nia pruned her face as she pointed to her cowlick.

"This thing is called a cowlick?" she said. "I hate this."

I laughed. My wife, Maria, didn't like hers either.

"What you consider an imperfection, someone else might think of as wonderful," I said.

"I don't know what's weirder, you staring at me, or you liking *cowlicks*," she said, "Kind of creepy."

"No, it's not," I said. "Freddy Krueger is creepy. Frankenstein is creepy. I'm—

"Frankenstein was misunderstood," she clarified.

"True. I'm surprised you've read that one," I said. "And Nabokov too? Impressive."

"Yeah, I can't stand kiddie teenage books—no offense to *Walter Whims*. I love reading."

"Bravo, you have a cell phone and the novel is still a form of entertainment for you!"

"Yes," she boasted.

I continued, "But my point is—

"I get it. You're not creepy," she conceded. "Where's your wife by the way?"

"She's dead," I said.

"Oh, I'm sorry."

It was clear that Nia had little to no experience with death. She didn't know what to say next, which I think is the most natural reaction when it comes to hearing such sad news.

"What's truly *creepy*," I said, "is outliving the woman I loved and vowed to spend the rest of my life with, then seeing an uncanny resemblance in the hair of a fourteen-year-old runaway sitting across from me on the way to Budapest."

"Runaway?"

"Yes, it appears so."

Nia said nothing for a few minutes.

She eventually broke the silence by asking: "Do you think I'm pretty?"

"Well, yes," I said.

"So there *is* a Lolita thing," she said with a smirk.

"No, I'm sorry to disappoint you."

"That's a good thing, but..."

Nia's pregnant pause hinted at the insecurity of her fragile teenage self, intelligent, but already used to being propped up by superficial comments from the opposite sex.

"Nia, I see you like I would my grandchild—pretty and adorable in a non-creepy way," I said, using her own words, hoping to be better understood.

"Oh."

She seemed to be at a loss.

"In fact, I could be your great-grandpa," I said.

"Is that why you're helping me?"

"Past tense: Helped. I helped you in that one horrible moment," I said. "Now I'm keeping you company until we get to Budapest."

"And then?" Nia asked.

"And then I'll advise you to contact your parents and explain exactly where you are."

"I can't do that," she said matter-of-factly.

Her conviction was clear. Instead of explaining, she grabbed her book and covered her face with it. It was the first time I noticed what she was reading: *The Count of Monte Cristo*.

I recalled dealing with my own teenage daughter long ago, as well as former students, who were hell bent on not opening up. I realized that asking *why* she had run away from her parents and her country, and why she was travelling alone wouldn't get me anywhere. I'd already tried that.

I waited a few minutes until I came up with something.

"So why did you escape from that island prison, Edmund Dantes?"

She lowered the book, placed it on her lap, and glared at me.

"What?"

"There must be a reason," I said. "Is it to seek vengeance? Or to find your lost love?

The shocked expression on Nia's face was priceless.

"You've read this book?" she said.

"It's one of my favorites."

NIA

That's when I told Kurt everything. How I left home. Why I left home. About me and Alex. About The Epic Devastation.

At first I felt kind of embarrassed to admit that I'd run away from home to get revenge on a trashy girl and meet a flakey boy and win him back, but as I explained it to Kurt the whole thing actually made more sense. Here's what I told him:

Alex was an eighth grader at my school last year. I was in seventh grade. I had a huge crush on him the entire year but he was, like, always dating the two prettiest girls in eighth grade. Terrified of being rejected, I didn't let him know I liked him until the end of the school year when I turned fourteen. Yeah, I was old for my grade, but so was he—already turned fifteen. I waited until after my birthday because I figured Alex would think I was too young for him before that. I loved that Alex was an older boy. (Kurt laughed at the idea of a fifteen-year old boy being called "older." I stuck my tongue out at him—that made him laugh more).

I didn't really *directly* tell Alex that I liked him. Anna did. She found out through a mutual friend that Alex had broken up with his girlfriend of three months, Maggie, and she jumped straight in. Anna came right over to my place and took a "hot"—her words, not mine—picture of us in short shorts and shared it with him.

Anna then wrote to Alex—because sometimes she was more fearless than me—that there were "two sexy girls in the photo but only one was available."

Anna and I were stuck to the screen waiting for his response.

A minute later he wrote: "I assume you're talking about Nia."

He knows my name! I thought. *And he uses the word "assume," so he's not a dumb cutie!*

"Bingo!" Anna wrote back. "What do you think of Nia?"

It was risky. My chest constricted as I waited for his words to appear on the screen.

"She's cute... I mean, she's beautiful, really... but I don't know if she's into me."

What?! Ohmygod! I grabbed the phone out of Anna's hands and wrote, "She is! She likes you! She's had a crush on you all year!"

Giggling, Anna ripped her phone back to stop me from embarrassing myself. She deleted the crush-all-year confession and then sent it.

Waiting for his response was torture. I was actually shaking in anticipation.

"I can't take this," I told Anna, and walked out onto my dad's balcony. The skyline of Sofia looks pretty at sunset. Everything was green and the air was finally warm after a long winter. *Alex thinks I'm beautiful?* It was hard to believe, but I knew then that my year-long dream might come true: *Alex will be my boyfriend!*

The glass door opened and Anna emerged with a big grin on her face.

"You have a date!" She announced it like the milestone it was.

"What?!"

"You're meeting him on Saturday, in Doctor's Garden park at five."

"You're amazing, Anna!" I squealed and hugged her.

Our first date happened on June 21st, the Saturday after our last week of school. I probably changed my clothes twenty times before deciding to just be myself and go with my standard: Chuck Taylor Converse shoes, tight dark jeans, and a band T-shirt (Nirvana, on that particular day). Anna helped me with my make-up and walked with me to the edge of the park. We were already ten minutes late.

"Okay, you're on your own from here," she said. "Better to look independent."

That's when some kind of nausea hit me. My legs got wobbly and my feet didn't want to move.

"I can't breathe," I told her.

"Come on, Nia," Anna said, giving me a push. "He's gonna love you."

I strolled into the park as confidently as I could, masking my nerves and fear of rejection. But once I saw Alex on that bench, saw his cute dimpled smile, and how he stood up to hug me hello, my fear melted away. The hug shot a wave of sensual energy through my entire body. He was so close to me I could smell his hair—*coconut-scented shampoo, for sure.*

"You look amazing," Alex said.

"You, too," I said without thinking.

"Wanna walk and talk?" he asked.

I'd rather keep hugging you and then make-out all day.

"Sure," I said.

Talking to Alex was surprisingly easy. It turned out we had a lot in common.

We both criticised our private school for its fake image and hypocrisy.

We both disliked Mr Conrad, Maggie (his ex), and chalga music.

We both loved Nirvana, the Rolling Stones, The Clash, and Outkast.

And we both had crushes on each other earlier in the year!

When he told me he had a crush on me, my heart beat like a hyperactive bass drum. I admitted the same to him. It occurred to me to ask if he'd had a crush on me while he had a girlfriend, but I didn't want to ruin anything. Actually, we probably would have kissed at that moment, but it was strange timing. Too many people were around, we hadn't held hands yet, and the sun hadn't even set.

There were only two awkward parts of our first date. Right after he bought me some gelato, we were talking about movies with badass heroes. I mentioned Jason Bourne. He made a reference to Katniss Everdeen in the Hunger Games. I told him that I loved that book, but didn't like the movie as much, though I agreed that Katniss was a badass in both. I went into how *Hunger Games* was my favorite book in fifth grade, but then *The Book Thief* took over first place in sixth grade. I was about midway through my opinion of Ponyboy in *The Outsiders* when I realized I was babbling.

"Sorry for rambling," I said. "What's your favorite book?

He gave me a blank look. No response. *Was he in deep thought? Was it a bad question?*

"Um, I don't really have one," he said.

Immediately, I felt like a dork.

The only other awkward part was when we said goodbye. I wanted to kiss him but didn't want to make it obvious or desperate. My stomach was in knots and I felt all constricted and weird like I had before seeing him that day. He asked me what I was doing that summer, the next week, the next day, but I was too focused on his lips. *Was he gonna give me a big, long kiss, or just a peck, or nothing?*

Alex moved in with his arms extended. Damn it, just a hug. But this hug was big, warm, and felt amazing—so much that I let out a moan.

"Are you okay," he asked. "Was that too hard?"

"No, it was... exceptional," I said. *"Exceptional"? What kind of a girl says a hug is "exceptional"?*

"I'll text you later," he said, flashed his dimple, and turned away.

I skipped home like I was floating. *Did that really just happen? Did I really just have a date with Alex Dimov?*

On our second date, June 23rd, we went to the movies and he told me he liked me and we officially became boyfriend and girlfriend. When we sat down to watch *Fast and Furious* (which I didn't want to see but couldn't care less about) he laced his fingers through mine and we held hands the entire movie. Toward the end, right after Vin Diesel said one of his lame one-liners, we kissed. I mean, real kissing. And we kept kissing until the credits started rolling. Yeah, it was amazing. Bliss.

The last week of June, Alex was on vacation in Greece with his parents, but for all of July we saw each other almost every day. It was like heaven, my dream come true. Then, two weeks before school started, on August 20th, he told me two earth-shattering things:

1. He loved me, and...

2. He was moving to a boarding school in London in a week because his parents didn't like his attitude or his grades or his Bulgarian friends.

Enter Epic Devastation, Part One. The news sent conflicting shockwaves through me—to hear that a boy "loved me" and was leaving me in the span of thirty seconds! I cried. But Alex didn't cry. He gave me silver hoop earrings and said he was sorry. I was really confused, but then he kissed me and I told him that I loved him too.

It was all downhill from there.

Alex left a week later. He sent me some cute messages the first two weeks he was gone, you know, like "Miss you, Wanna kiss you," and "You're my little chicken" (Trust me, it sounds cute in Bulgarian). But then the sweet messages stopped coming. I sent him a few metaphorical messages about bringing sunshine to the cloudy UK if I came to visit him, but his responses became very short, even rude. Like one time when he wrote "Dream on ☺." *What the hell did that mean? Was he trying to be funny, referring to the Aerosmith song, or just being a jerk?* Anyway, he pissed me off and made me feel really insecure. I didn't want to be super needy and obsessed so I stopped sending him messages, hoping he would miss me and call or text.

But, no. Nothing.

Enter Epic Devastation, Part Two.

I admit it, I got totally paranoid and obsessive. I entered full-on stalkerdom by checking his social media profiles every hour, looking for clues as to what he was doing or thinking. For a week there was nothing, no signs that anything was different. Then I began to notice that the same girl, *Victoria*, was making comments on all his pictures. First they were snarky, trying-to-be-funny comments, then they started to sound flirty like, "OMG Handsome"—even intimate like, "I see my favorite dimple!" I friended her under a false name and began stalking her profile, too. That's when I realized that Victoria—Victoria Pavlova was her name—had gone to my school in Sofia two years before. She was in Alex's class and had won every academic and athletic award possible back when I was in sixth grade. Not to mention she was freaking beautiful. I was jealous of her then. Now I hated her.

Well, *hate* is a strong word. I didn't officially hate her until she posted a picture of her and Alex in the lobby of her preppy boarding school in England (their schools were only twenty kilometers away from each other). They were hugging and her face was pressed up next to his with the caption "my new love." Not only did it make me want to vomit, it made me angrier than I've ever felt in my life. Alex had just proclaimed his love for me a month before and then it was over so easily? He'd moved on right after me—*or worse*—I swiped through hundreds of photos on their profiles and found a new piece of damning evidence: a selfie of their faces smushed together at a popular festival in Sofia that was always the first week in August!

Epic Devastation, Part Three:

Alex had started cheating on me with Victoria in Bulgaria while we were still together! As all the disgusting possibilities flooded my mind and sickened my heart, I plotted ways to get back at both of them—to ruin their "new love." *But how could it be "love" with her when he loved me?* It sparked a ton of questions, but only one answer became clear to me: I wanted vengeance and I wanted it to really hurt. All the options flooded in: messaging them directly, sending her pictures of Alex and I, or maybe even fabricating some story to make them both hate each other.

The only problem was that I still loved Alex. Yeah, I actually wanted to get him back. I thought that if he and I lived in the same place, we would still be together and none of The Epic Devastation would have happened. Though I was furious, I still believed that he "loved" me, that I wasn't just some random girl to him. We'd had so much fun that summer going to the movies, kissing in the park, and laughing just because. Honestly, it was the happiest time of my life.

Was all of it a big fat lie?

No, it wasn't possible.

It might sound stupid, but after weeks of no communication in September, I sent him a message with no text—just a purple heart emoji. I waited for a response all night until I couldn't keep my eyes open any longer. The next morning I woke up to his equally simple but no less powerful text: "NC2U." It took me a few seconds to figure it out. It was our song that summer: *Nothing Compares to You*! We had heard it at the mall once and he started singing the chorus to me. His voice was horrible, but it was the words, the effort, the romantic part that I loved.

All that morning I was on a high, thinking about re- uniting with Alex and listening to Sinead O'Connor's pretty voice on repeat, until I checked Victoria's post. It was another mushy pic of them together, and this time she was kissing him. The caption read: "Can't wait to rendezvous with my man next weekend!" #schooltrip #radissonhotel #berlin."

My man?! A hotel?!

I boiled with rage. It was clear why there was so much violence in the world.

I *had* to do something.

It might sound crazy, but it was because of this post, the NC2U text, along with the fact that I was reading the *Count of Monte Cristo*—the story of an escape and mission to seek revenge and find lost love—that I came up with the idea to run away from my parents, take a train to Berlin and confront Alex and Victoria in person at the Radisson Hotel that Saturday.

When I finished explaining, I realized I had rambled to Kurt for twenty minutes, nonstop. For a second or two, he just sat there speechless.

KURT

"Holy cow," I said, "Aside from the fact that your parents must be worried sick, you've got a helluva story cookin."

"My parents aren't worried sick, I assure you," she said.

"Why is that?"

"They hate me," Nia said.

"Impossible."

"Okay, they don't like me or care about me, how's that?"

"Highly unlikely," I said.

"Then where are they now?" Nia asked, rhetorically.

"In Bulgaria, I presume, where you left them."

"Yeah, well, I can make some presumptions too!" Nia claimed. "Sometime between tonight and tomorrow, my parents will finally come to the conclusion that their only child is missing. My dad will assume, because he never talks to my mom, that I am with her. My mom will assume, because she never talks to my dad, that I'm with him. Soon they will be forced to speak to each other about my disappearance, which will probably be reported to them by my anal-retentive school. My parents will think that I've been kidnapped because they couldn't fathom any other option—unless my dad notices the 500 euros missing from his not-so-secret hiding spot. They will tell the police that they know their daughter well, and that her running away is not a possibility. The truth is that they don't know me at all. Not a clue."

Nia was visibly worked up—which is why I shouldn't have said:

"Sounds pretty normal to me."

"What?" she belted out.

"You're a teenager, so you most likely created some distance," I said, holding my right hand up in front of me, fingers extended, signaling my desire to finish my thought without being interrupted. "Parents sense the change and they usually don't know how to deal with teenagers all cranked up on hormones, so they avoid them. It's sad but common."

"It's abuse," she fired back. "Complete neglect is abuse."

"That's a strong word," I said.

Nia re-positioned herself in her chair and changed her tack.

"I know it was a long time ago, but did your parents ever make you breakfast or dinner when you were a kid?"

"Of course," I said.

"Helped you with homework?" she asked.

"Yes, I believe so."

"Helped you get dressed before school?"

"I'm afraid that's a bit too long ago to remember," I admitted.

"Well, my parents have never done any of those things, ever," Nia said.

"Ever?"

"Ever."

"Really?"

"All they've done is argue, slam doors, throw things at each other and yell at me to go to my room, do my homework or watch a movie, or go to my friend's house. Now they're divorced, so they live in separate places and never talk. I've only had Nona, my nanny, since I can remember. She does all the things my parents are supposed to do. She even talks to me sometimes, but not much—probably because it's not in her contract to talk to me. She doesn't get paid for it."

I didn't know what to say at first. I was not used to hearing this kind of problem: Rich kid problems. I had never been rich or been friends with anyone who was. Perhaps that's why I never had much sympathy for the ridiculously wealthy, but seeing the pain in Nia's face made me empathize. She was truly unhappy, despite her luxury world (she later mentioned that her parents have separate penthouse apartments in Sofia, a beach house on the Black Sea, a chateau in Bansko, and apartments in downtown Rome and Paris).

"What about birthday parties?" I ignorantly added.

"Oh my God, how did you know!? They didn't even *go* to my last birthday party. But they threw gifts at me—

literally. They think that will somehow make up for the fact that they don't talk to me, don't show up, and avoid me. But I know that they don't really care!"

She almost started to cry, but held back the tears.

"I'm sorry to hear that," I said. "They really didn't show up, huh?"

"My mom dropped me off and said she'd come later on," Nia explained. "Then an hour later she sent me a text saying she had important business."

"Hmm."

"My dad said he would come, then texted that he'd be late, never showed up, then sent his driver to pick me up because he had a 'million-dollar meeting.'"

"Ouch," I said.

"Yeah, I mean, how much am I worth to him?" she said. "Obviously a lot less than a million dollars!"

I had pity for the kid. She had youth and wealth, but no love, no sense of support—the most important things. Sounded like her parents didn't know Nia in the slightest, and hadn't tried too hard to figure her out or show any affection. Despite her naïve impulsivity and long list of bad decisions, it seemed that Nia had run away for fairly decent reasons.

I was so fascinated by listening to Nia's escape story, I'd lost track of time. When I checked my watch it was almost 2 a.m., we were nearing the Hungarian border, and there was an attempted rapist either unconscious where we'd left him or roaming the train in search of the old fart who'd knocked him out. My neck and back were killing me, and I hadn't had more than five minutes of sleep.

NIA

After I told Kurt way more about The Epic Devastation and my parents than I'd planned to, he suggested that we rest for a while. I read instead. I couldn't go back to sleep and neither could he. Edmond Dantes was in the middle of getting his revenge on Mondego at his villa in Paris when we were startled by three loud knocks on our cabin door. I jumped a little and looked up from my book as the door was jostled open and a pair of stocky Hungarian border officers entered. Their uniforms had that intimidating military look. One officer had a menacing brow and the other a thick, creepy mustache. It was the second time that night I felt truly scared.

Menacing Brow said something in what I presume was Hungarian.

Creepy Mustache Guy said, "English?"

"Yes, we speak English," Kurt said.

From that point on, Creepy Mustache Guy did the talking in broken English and Menacing Brow, well, he looked menacing and didn't say much. I was too frightened to speak, worried that the unconscious rapist guy or my running away had already somehow been discovered.

Creepy Mustache Guy asked a ton of questions in broken English, like:

"Where to you from?"

"How many days you traveling?"

"You make change of seats on train?"

"To what address you go in Budapest?"

"You are travel together? Family?"

Kurt answered most of them smoothly, whether true or not, except for the last one. He hesitated. That's when I told the officers, "He's my great-grandfather."

Kurt glanced at the Creepy Mustache Guy and nodded.

The strange thing was that Menacing Brow looked through some of Kurt's stuff. Then he grabbed my bag and rummaged through it. He eyed the cash as if it were illegal for me to have hundreds of euros. He also picked up and examined Kurt's cane which freaked me out. *Why check out an old man's cane so curiously?* Even Kurt, usually flatline-calm, took notice.

They checked both of our passports for longer than expected. Again, I feared a premature ending—getting caught, stopped dead in my tracks if my parents had caught on to me. They or my school might have already alerted the authorities to be on the lookout for Nia Mladenova at all international borders in Europe. My father had big connections, my mom too. But after fingering through my passport pages for a few minutes, Creepy Mustache Guy shrugged and handed it back.

Menacing Brow asked Kurt something in Hungarian and Kurt shook his head, having no clue what the man said.

When they left, I exhaled as if I'd been holding my breath the whole time.

"Kurt," I said, "Do you think they know anything?"

"Know what?" he asked.

"Know about the rapist guy!"

"Keep your voice down," Kurt said, composed again. "If they don't yet, then they will soon enough—unless he's recovered and wandered off to some seat in another part of the train, or got off at one of the stops. Who knows, he might have gained consciousness but has no memory of being hit."

"Or, he's very mad and wants to kill both of us," I added.

"Perhaps."

Kurt was impossibly relaxed. I was the opposite.

"Why do you sound like you don't care?"

"Because I'm too old to worry," he said.

"Seriously?"

"Nia," he said, "If they come back here and ask us questions about a hairy bastard with a large head wound, then we should be honest. Otherwise, remain silent."

He said *remain silent* in a way you might expect from a villain in the movies. It made me wonder about the old man for the first time since we'd met. After all, I had only known him for a grand total of three hours.

61

"Kurt, can I ask you a question?" I said.

When he responded with a nod, I suddenly got nervous.

I peered up at the ceiling as if random interview questions were written on post-its and I just had to choose one to ask. That would have been easy, but I really had only one question in mind. Kurt had a polite expression on his face as if I was going to ask something like: *Where are you from originally? How old are you? How many kids and grandkids do you have? What was the inspiration behind the character Walter Whims?*

And then I asked:

"Have you ever killed anyone before?"

KURT

Nia caught me off guard. That was a helluva question. It was strange that she asked it, but so was everything about that night.

"Yes."

I said this after a few moments of hesitation and thought. "Yes, I have killed someone."

"Um..." Nia responded with wide eyes. This information seemed to alarm her.

"It was during the war, years ago," I said.

"World War I?" she asked, "or Vietnam?"

I laughed, remembering my teaching days when kids regularly displayed their lack of historical timeline and any sense of older peoples' age. I was ancient to them, so I could've fought in the Trojan War for God's sake. The Vietnam War could've happened before the Civil War as far as they were concerned.

"World War II," I said.

"Wow," Nia said. "How did it happen?"

I explained to her that I was only 17 when I signed up for the US army. I lied and told the recruiters that I was 18 and, believe it or not, they didn't ask any questions.

Throughout basic training I was so happy to be passing as an "adult" and becoming a "real soldier" that I didn't give a thought to the idea that over half of my unit would soon be sent to their graves.

On the way over to Europe we worried about two things: being killed and having to kill others.

It was on our second overcast day of trekking in western Germany that my platoon—a group of kids with guns, really—came upon the small town of Jesberg. I will never forget the name because as we approached on foot, we thought the sign that said "Jesberg" and the little white houses were so quaint, seemingly untouched by the war. The peaceful town didn't fit or make any sense.

Our sergeant met an older man in the otherwise empty main street and asked if the US Army could use any of the unoccupied houses for shelter that night. The balding German man seemed nice enough, but all he did was point to a vacant barn-like building. Two hours later, we'd completely commandeered the place, lit up cigarettes, made coffee, and were chewing on beef jerky.

We had four guys guarding the perimeter at dusk.

They were shot first.

We were naive enough to think that we were safe behind enemy lines and that the German man who had directed us to our makeshift home was not a Nazi sympathizer.

Turned out, he was.

When gunfire opened up on our position, sounding like a string of firecrackers, it didn't take long to realize that we were surrounded. Bullets streamed into the room from multiple angles. Chaos ensued. The blonde guy from Kansas that happened to be standing by the window closest to me was mowed down to a lifeless lump on the floor. I dropped to the ground and kept my head low like the others. Mitch, a big Italian guy from Chicago, was right next to me.

"We need to get outta' here before this whole place is blown to bits," he said.

I agreed.

Mitch was the kind of guy you trusted straight away.

"If we sneak out the back, there's some trees we can use for cover," Mitch said. "Grab your gun and crawl behind me."

I followed him to the back door.

"This is either genius, or the dumbest move of our lives," he said.

I agreed.

Mitch shot one German hidden directly behind the building before I'd even poked my head out the door.

"Follow me!" he said.

We ran straight in the direction of the German he'd just shot. All I heard was the clacking of gunshots and the whizzing of bullets piercing air. It was maybe twenty meters, a few seconds of running, but it felt like we ran the length of a football field. When we got to the dead German, we crouched next to him and Mitch flipped him over. Damned if it wasn't the same old man who had directed us to that barn. This old Nazi couldn't have been under sixty years old, so the barn might not have been surrounded by regular Nazi soldiers, but Jesbergers of all ages.

Mitch scanned the area with his rifle ready at his shoulder. He was a damned good marksman. He locked in on someone off to the left of the barn, in a clearing beyond the trees.

"*Spetta*," he whispered in Italian—his only warning before firing a shot that left the victim face down in the grass.

"Nice shot," I said.

There was an eerie pause in the shooting. Then the right half of the barn—where we'd all been casually hanging out just five minutes earlier—blew up. I immediately fell to my knees after the blast, thinking that my entire platoon had been blown to smithereens. Mitch poked his head out from behind the tree to get a better assessment of the damage.

That's when someone blew Mitch's head off. Just like that.

Of course, his head didn't come clean off, but the shot took out a big chunk of his head. It was grotesque—by far the most disgusting thing I'd ever seen. He fell backward like a puppet whose puppeteer had suddenly run away. It was the most frightening moment of my life. I was completely alone and as good as dead.

Seconds later, I heard someone approaching through the tall grass. I was shaking, too afraid to look. I held my pistol tight with my finger near the trigger and stayed low behind the base of a thick tree. I could hear that the approaching man had stopped short of Mitch's dead body.

He was very close, maybe ten feet away from me.

I heard him mutter something to himself in German and that was my cue. I popped out from behind the tree with my pistol pointed at him. I remember the shock on this blonde German's face. He was a kid—maybe sixteen, seventeen. My age. He could have been my classmate for God's sake. I'd caught him with his rifle down at his side. I could only assume he had just killed Mitch.

The German remained frozen for a few long seconds, then began to say something in his native tongue, and that's when I placed my finger on the trigger and shot him.

I didn't mean to. My intention was to ready myself, not actually shoot, but the trigger was extra sensitive. I'd never fired that particular pistol before.

As the German kid fell to the ground, I ducked and looked around to see if any others were nearby and then darted into the woods, away from the barn, the town, all the dead bodies.

Shots were being fired in the distance, but I kept running like hell through a field until I had made it to a wooded area on a hill. It couldn't have been more than a mile away. I perched myself on the highpoint of that hill, under the cover of some brush, and was too frightened to move until the next day when the US infantry marched into Jesberg, searched the surrounding area, and found me half-frozen.

I was saved, but everyone else in my platoon was dead.

It took me longer than I thought to tell the story. I expected Nia to be dozing off by the time I finished, but she was wide awake.

"That's crazy," Nia said.

"Not really," I told her. "It was common at the time. Far worse happened. I got lucky and survived."

"I've never seen a dead body before," Nia said.

"Be patient, you have time," I said.

I thought it was kind of funny but she didn't laugh.

"I figure there are two ways to deal with our tragic world," I told her. "Either laugh or cry about it. With laughter there's much less cleanup."

She gave me a sassy smirk.

"If you were in World War II, then how old are you?" Nia asked.

"Eighty-nine," I said.

NIA

I knew Kurt was like, *old*, but I didn't realize he was truly ancient until he told that war story. I mean, World War II happened in the *1940s*! *He'd fought against Hitler!*

At that point, two things became clear to me:

> 1. Neither of us was falling asleep before getting to Budapest, and...

> 2. Kurt might *literally* die of old age at any moment.

Because I was reading *The Count of Monte Cristo*, I started to think of Kurt as old Faria in prison with Edmond Dantes. He taught him so much and gave him the map, then his death gave Dantes the ability to escape from that awful prison, *Chateau d'If*. But I was starting to like Kurt and didn't want to think of him dying, so I also thought of him as the character Jacopo instead. Jacopo is the friend who helped Dantes with his plans to seek vengeance and justice for those who'd betrayed him. I skimmed back to a part I had underlined on page 120:

> *"I desire to live, to fight till the end. I wish to reconquer the happiness that has been taken from me."*

And that's when I really started thinking of myself as a young, female Edmond Dantes. Yes, I was seeking justice. Alex had taken my happiness. Victoria had swooped in and was making it ten times worse, taking advantage of Alex—away from home for the first time, clearly disoriented (as evidenced by the NC2U text) and disconnected from his normal self. All this while I was far away, stuck in my Bulgarian luxury *Chateau d'If*. I could just picture Victoria's strong-willed and dominating personality prying Alex away from me. Of course, Alex wasn't entirely guilt-free. He probably thought that Victoria was a sophisticated, hot, older girl (she was sixteen) and he was weak enough to fall for the next best thing. But that's why I could forgive him, too. We had been forcibly separated. I could remind him that he loved me and send Victoria packing—embarrassed and destroyed—by planning the perfect Monte Cristo confrontation at the Radisson in Berlin.

Thinking of getting back at Alex made me picture being with him that blissful summer. We always sat on that same bench where we first met in Doctor's Garden. It was our special meeting spot—our kissing spot. His hair always smelled like coconut and his shirts like he'd sprayed too much of his dad's Tom Ford cologne on. But I didn't really care about that. I loved his lips, the sound of his voice, and the way he looked at me.

Alex told me how pretty I was, that he loved my hair, that my green eyes were gorgeous. I remember playing with my hair and giggling a lot at his superficial compliments. I remember telling him about my annoying parents, what I had been reading, and stories of my friendship with Anna. He mostly talked about his friends and basketball. He never said *why* he enjoyed spending time with me, or talked about our future, or mentioned *a thing* about moving away from Bulgaria—not once.

That hadn't occurred to me before. *Didn't you have to apply to those boarding schools way in advance? Or was it not planned and he just wanted to get away from me, or someone else?* This sparked a series of other troubling questions: *Why else would he leave so abruptly? Why didn't he tell me anything about it? What else did he lie to me about?* And then there was the whole Victoria thing. *When exactly had that started? Had we kissed Alex on the same day? Gag. Did she think she was better than me? Did she even know about me? Did he ever really love me? And what was it that made me love him?*

All these thoughts led me to an epic question: Did I really even *know* Alex? Kind of an important one if I was traveling over a thousand kilometers and breaking laws for him, right?

After thinking it over, I felt like I'd found out more about Kurt in three hours than I had learned about Alex in two months.

KURT

That night seemed never ending. It must have been five a.m. as we neared Budapest. My bones were so sore all I could think about was lying down. I decided to check into my hotel room as soon as I arrived and to sleep well into the afternoon. I didn't share my plan with Nia, because I figured it would be easiest to say goodbye when we naturally parted at the train station. As I envisioned my day in Budapest—mostly dreaming of sleep, but also picturing the Danube and recalling fond memories—Nia lowered her book from her eyes to her lap.

She asked me with no beating-around-the-bush:

"Why are *you* on this train, Kurt?"

"I'm also on a journey to *mi amore*."

"What?" Nia said, confused.

"The short answer is: to visit Maria, my wife," I said.

"I thought she was dead."

"Exactly."

"I don't get it," Nia said.

"Well, maybe I should clarify."

"Please."

I told Nia that in the late spring of 1945 I was moved to Budapest. Of course, there were mostly Russians helping rebuild Budapest, but I guess they wanted a small American presence there, too. There was still tension in the air because the Russians were setting up shop and the Hungarians didn't know when the excrement would hit the fan again, so to speak.

Every morning I would walk by a smart little bakery on Vaci Street. Some buildings were still boarded up or bombed out, so this unscarred bakery stood out. The very first time I passed, I glanced in the window and noticed her dark brown hair. Of course, I didn't know her name nor had I even seen her face clearly. I just imagined her as the pretty brunette in the bakery.

After about four days of timidly passing by, I decided to go inside, buy some bread, and meet this girl. I must have taken her by surprise because she seemed a bit put off by my entrance. She was reserved and almost expressionless. It wasn't until I bought a loaf of bread and greeted her that she smiled at me. She brushed her hair back, her smile widened, and her eyes lit up. She was gorgeous. I noticed her cowlick cutely placed on her hairline. I was so mesmerized that I couldn't speak. She said something to me in Hungarian and I had no idea what it meant. When English came out of my mouth she giggled, but said nothing.

I felt awkward and embarrassed by the language barrier so I waved to her and left. That night I studied some basic Hungarian phrases. When I returned to see her the next morning, the only one I remembered was: *Hogy hívnak?* — "What's your name?" She said "Maria." That was it. I bought two croissants to look like a legitimate customer and continued on my way to work.

Every day for two weeks, I repeated this. I'd learn a new Hungarian phrase at night, use it the next morning, she would giggle, and I would continue onto work. Just when I became convinced that she knew absolutely no English, one day she asked me my name. Then she asked how I was and why I was in Budapest. Turned out her English was ten times better than my Hungarian! That same day I asked her if she'd have dinner with me. She said no, but by the following morning she'd changed her mind. Maria and I walked along the Danube that night, gazing at the stars, using charade-like sign language, and laughing at each other.

At first, our communication was primitive, but after a few more weeks we'd made progress—her English improved much faster than my Hungarian. We held hands, kissed, and strolled along that river every night, but didn't go beyond this innocent kind of courting because that was normal back in those days and she seemed guarded. I was just delighted to be around her. So, weeks later when I was informed that the Russians were aggressively taking over all rebuilding duties and I would be shipped back to America, I faced a dilemma. I didn't want to leave Maria. Actually, I couldn't imagine spending a day without her.

To her mother's disbelief, I proposed marriage and asked if Maria would come back to the US with me a week later. I was hoping she'd hug me, kiss me, and say yes. Instead, Maria cried. She played with a strand of her unforgettable hair and told me she had to think about it. After three days of waiting for her response, feeling like my exposed heart was being dragged across cold gravel, she said yes!

Never in a million years could I have pictured myself returning to Budapest as a crumbling old man, set on paying my love and respect to Maria's gravestone.

PART II: Budapest

NIA

Our train arrived in Budapest as the sun was coming up. I tried to help Kurt by carrying his one small travel bag but he stubbornly resisted. In a half-asleep, unclean zombie state, I put on my favorite jacket, grabbed my backpack, and worried about where the rapist guy might be.

"Kurt," I started, "about that creep you knocked out with your cane...?"

"For now, we'll pretend like it didn't happen," he said.

"But I'm a little worried—

"No point in worrying about something going wrong until you actually know something has gone wrong," he said. "Worrying won't help unless it involves some kind of real plan."

Thanks, Kurt.

That reminded me that I had *no real plan* once I arrived in Budapest. I had done my research and knew there was a night train from Budapest to Berlin, but between that morning and eleven o'clock that night, I had no plan. I just assumed Kurt would stick with me because he was now like a grandpa figure—my savior grandpa—but as soon as we stepped off the train and onto the platform he turned to me.

"I guess this is goodbye, Nia."

"What?"

I was surprised. I mean, I don't know exactly what I expected, but at least he would make sure I had a place to go, or ask me to come with him and grab a cappuccino, or offer some help—*something, right?*

"I thought we were partners," I said, which sounded lame and pathetic as soon as it came out.

"Oh, Nia, I'm sorry to disappoint you," Kurt said, "Sometimes the journey comes to an end before you know it."

"I guess so," I said. I didn't want to appear weak.

"And you're not the only one on a mission," he added.

Kurt's voice sounded weird, more hollow and feeble than usual. His eyes were glazed over and bloodshot. I probably looked like crap, too. As I stood there speechless and semi-awake, he wished me luck and gave me one last piece of advice.

"Nia, do me a favor," he said. "Find a safe place and call your parents as soon as possible. I'm sure they're worried sick."

"I doubt it."

"Think about it," Kurt said, "They love you."

Honestly, I assumed that my parents still didn't even know I was missing. Part of me wanted to plead with Kurt and ask him for help, but I also wasn't even sure why I felt like I needed him. After all, I had started this journey expecting to be solo.

I wanted adventure.

I wanted to be Edmund Dantes...

But I was scared to death.

Kurt gave me a kind smile and a pat on the shoulder, turned and walked away. I stood there, abandoned, watching him go. He moved slowly, his back hunched right below the neck. He dragged his feet a bit and favored his left leg so much that he basically walked with a limp. His bag was so small and seemingly empty, I wondered how he could pack more than a few toiletries and one change of clothes in that thing. Then I lost sight of him in the train station crowd.

Still standing on the platform like a lost puppy, two paramedics passed right by me. They were carrying a white-sheet-covered man on a stretcher. It was obviously a man because I noticed his cheap brown shoes hanging off the edge. *It could be the rapist guy*! And if he was being carried away on a stretcher, it meant he was dead.

I wanted to run away, but then I paused. *What would the Count of Monte Cristo do?* Since nobody ever recognized the Count (aka Edmund Dantes), he was bold enough to calmly confront the very people who posed the biggest danger to him. Since I was about as anonymous as anyone, I decided to ask one of the three paramedics about the man on the stretcher. I caught up to the third paramedic guy trailing behind. He had a red medical bag in his hand and a clipboard in the other.

"Excuse me, is the person they're carrying okay?" I asked in my best innocent-dumb-kid voice.

"This is not your concern," the paramedic said with a thick Hungarian accent.

I hesitated, but couldn't leave it at that.

"Um, I'm here to pick up my old uncle with diabetes and I'm worried he might be..." I pointed to the stretcher.

"This man not your uncle," he affirmed.

"How do you know?"

"Not die from diabetic problem and not old," he said stoically.

"He's dead?" I asked.

"Yes."

That's when the guy I was talking to bumped into the back of his paramedic partner holding the stretcher. That little bump made the platform jerk and out fell the limp, hairy hand of the dead man underneath the sheet. I gasped. On the finger of that hand was the smelly silver ring that had practically been shoved up my nose. It was the rapist guy, for sure.

Confirmed: Kurt had killed him.

Panicked, I ran off in the direction I had last seen Kurt go. I rushed into the main part of the old-fashioned station, looked around frantically, and couldn't see him anywhere. When I stopped to get my bearings, I turned around and saw the paramedics pointing at me as if they suspected *me* now and wanted to ask questions. This only heightened my panic. I ran out to the street. *Shit, I am in Budapest! I know nothing about this city.* I needed help. I figured Kurt couldn't have gotten very far, nor would he want to walk much.

Taxis! I looked around the square and saw a line of taxis parked against the far sidewalk and Kurt getting into one. The boulevard was wide, but I darted across the intersection and ran up to Kurt's taxi just as it pulled away. I glanced back at the train station and saw two paramedics and a police officer scanning the area. *Were they looking for me?* Freaked out, I turned and walked briskly in the direction Kurt's taxi was heading.

I spotted his yellow cab stopped at a light a block ahead. I wanted to sprint up to it and tell him about the dead rapist guy, but I didn't want to run because the police or paramedics would easily spot me. So I walked fast and almost caught up to the taxi, anyway. When the taxi stopped at the next traffic light, I wondered if I might catch up to it again—and was amazed that even without traffic, walking could be almost as fast as driving in the heart of a big city. When I was within fifty meters of the taxi and far enough away from the train station, I finally ran toward the intersection as the light turned green. It seemed hopeless, but I kept running anyway, pretending I was some kind of character in a Marvel movie who had special powers.

Except my super powers weren't working—the taxi pulled away. I was feeling the weight of my backpack and the lack of sleep. Yet I kept running. For blocks I tried to keep my eye on the taxi as it distanced itself from me. My eyes tracked it all the way onto a bridge that crossed a river, and then I lost sight of it. By the time I made it to that river I was completely exhausted. I turned around and no one seemed to be following me.

I rested my arms on the short wall that lined the river's edge and gazed across it. The bridge itself, the lion sculpture, and the view on the opposite bank were stunning in the early morning light, but I focused on the road on the other side of the river and the few cars on it— one of them a taxi. I watched it continue to the left, past another bridge and then out of sight. I imagined that taxi stopping in front of a hotel along the river, and Kurt getting out of it.

Imagined.

Face it Nia, you have no clue.

You're all alone now.

I dropped my head into my hands in despair and cried.

Why did I feel so abandoned? I never expected a travel companion.

Feeling vulnerable, cold, and not wanting to look like an easy target, I wiped the tears away and walked along the river in search of a safe place. I tried to follow Kurt's advice to not worry, but it didn't really work.

KURT

There were a few reasons why that taxi ride to the Art'Otel was so great. One, it was along the Danube, a river that brings back the best memories. Two, I knew I would soon be able to rest my old bones on a comfortable bed. Three, I'd stayed at the Art'Otel before and expected the breakfast buffet would be excellent—thus I would first eat well, then sleep well. Four, I was on my own, back to my own plan and freed from the tension and drama of teenage Nia—who was clever and interesting in her own right, but whose generational frequency was quite different than mine. I was too exhausted to see that talking to her made my train trip much more intriguing—and she had distracted me from my arthritis and my painful thoughts.

Indeed, the buffet breakfast was excellent. I went to the room, took some of my senior citizen medication—a dozen pills per day—and planned to sleep like a baby. I put in a request with the hotel receptionist for a wake up call at 12 noon. It was a big day and I didn't want to sleep through all of it. I was set on visiting my beloved Maria as soon as possible.

NIA

Walking the empty early morning streets of Budapest gave me time to plan.

I could have taken a train to Vienna that afternoon, transferred, gone on to Prague, waited and transferred again, and arrived in Berlin later on that night, but it made no sense to me. I'd rather wait till the night train at nine p.m. that went all the way from Budapest to Berlin and sleep on the train (in a private cabin) instead of checking into a hotel in Berlin by myself—something a fourteen-year-old might not be able to do. Of course, the idea of sleeping on a train alone kind of freaked me out which was another reason I wanted to have Kurt with me. Aside from a sense of safety, I needed Kurt back because he would make traveling across borders easier, and also might be able to assist with my unformed plan to get back Alex and humiliate Victoria.

Not to mention that I felt it my duty to tell Kurt that he killed the rapist guy on the train and might be wanted for murder. But mostly, though I didn't want to admit it, I was scared and just wanted someone I trusted to be with me. This adventure was, so far, entirely different than what I had expected. I mean, it was fun to plan out my escape and it was exhilarating to actually leave Sofia, but then it went from being a boring train ride to a nightmarish attack—less Alexander Dumas and more Stephen King. Thank God for Kurt. No wonder I wanted to find him so bad. Yet another part of me still wanted to be independent, like Edmond Dantes. Yes, I was conflicted, frustrated, and tired.

I found a Costa Coffee shop that had just opened up. I ordered a cappuccino and claimed the big comfy chair nestled in the corner. Two young baristas went through the motions of cleaning and setting up for the day. It was empty and seemed like a safe place. Before touching my drink, I slouched and leaned my head on the wing of the chair and closed my eyes...

"Hallo."

Insert jumble of Hungarian words.

"Do you speak English?"

I woke up to the barista saying this, his hands close to my shoulder as if he were about to shake me. Skinny with longish hair and sparse beard, he looked like one of Jesus's young disciples.

I glanced around, not certain where I was at first.

"Oh my God, did I fall asleep?" I asked him.

"Yes, for maybe hour," he said and chuckled. "Would you like *melegítésére*—uhh, heat your cappuccino?"

"Yes, please. Thank you," I said, wiping the sleep from my eyes.

I went to the bathroom and checked myself in the mirror. I looked horrid, like I'd been in a fight. My eyes were puffy, my hair was a mess, and there was an imprint of the chair's seam on my cheek that made me look like Al Pacino in "Scarface." I washed my face, put on a little makeup, and returned to my chair.

I spent the next hour sipping my cappuccino and reading *Monte Cristo*. I slogged through the part where Dantes is in Paris, methodically ruining the lives of his enemies. Compared to his prison escape, finding the treasure, and plotting his revenge, these later chapters were kind of slow. I was on page 380 and still had 200 to get to the end! I was about to put the book down and give my eyes a rest when I made it to this line by the Count:

> *"I wish to be Providence myself, for I feel that the most beautiful, noblest, most sublime thing in the world, is to recompense and punish."*

It wasn't 100% me, but I liked his style. The Count was obsessed with rewarding those who'd been good to him and punishing the bad. But the way he did it was important. He didn't just go kill his enemies. He did background work and set them up so they would ultimately ruin—kill, go bankrupt or insane (or all of the above)—themselves. It was genius! It's what I wanted to do, in effect, to Alex and Victoria. I wanted to set up a situation that would humiliate them and make them feel horrible. But it wasn't going to come from me scolding them for cheating or lying. I had to figure out a way to hold a mirror up to them so they could realize how wrong they were.

Maybe that would also bring Alex to his senses and back to me.

Despite the fact that my nanny told me I was too young to drink coffee, I went to the counter and ordered another.

"Cafe Americano, please." I said.

The barista—the same guy who had woken me up—gave me a strange look. I assumed, like most Europeans, he was judging my Americano request as foolish—the best way to ruin a good coffee with way too much water. But that wasn't it.

"Are you not too young to drink so much coffee?" he asked.

"Excuse me?" I said, not in the mood to be questioned by anyone, much less an ESL boyish barista.

"How many years are you?" he asked.

"None of your business," I snapped back.

He examined me, in full judgment mode.

"And why are you not in school today?" he added.

"Oh, you're my dad now?" I said, not holding back on bitch mode. "No, wait. That's impossible because you can't be much older than eighteen, right?"

"Okay." Barista guy put his hands up to indicate he was backing off. "Calm down," he said.

"I am calm!" I yelled and put my five euro bill on the counter. "Can I just have my coffee, please?"

Barista guy gave me an evil eye. He had no idea how close I was to blowing up and crying for the second time that morning.

When he slid my coffee across the counter a minute later, he gave me a condescending smirk and said, "Be careful. It's hot."

I rolled my eyes and took the cup. Sure, I was being bitchy, but I couldn't help it. I hadn't slept much or showered in over twenty-four hours, it was still early in the morning, and this barista exposed my main weakness on this mission: I was a little too young to be on my own, much less to travel internationally.

I needed encouragement. I had to chat with Anna. Against my better judgment, I dug my phone out of my bag and turned it on. As soon as I entered my passcode, the screen filled with notifications: Nine missed calls from my dad. Twelve missed calls from my mom. One text from Anna that I read first.

ANNA: OMG, u r in deep shit, Nia! this is serious!!! Text me!!!

She'd sent it only an hour before. My mom's calls started at ten p.m. the night before, my dad's closer to eleven. I couldn't handle talking to either of them. It was too much. They'd be too angry to hear me out anyway. Texting Anna was my only option. According to my calculations, Anna would be finishing our first period English class soon.

NIA: whatsup?

Two minutes later...

ANNA: holy shit, Nia! Where r u? R u OK?

NIA: yeah, i'm fine. I'm in budapest...drinking coffee

ANNA: OMG! this is crazy. I got called into the principal's office this morning... with your parents!!! They questioned me so much i cried!!! ;(

NIA: OMG! I am soooo sorry... what do they know?

ANNA: at first they thought u were kidnapped!...i told them u probably ran away, but said i didn't know anything.

NIA: and they believed u?!

ANNA: they didn't... they think i'm lying and that u have no reason to run away... so i told them how upset u were that they missed your birthday...

NIA: and...?

ANNA: and they didn't listen. They r convinced u were kidnapped!!!!...now you r considered "MISSING"!!!... the police r searching for u!!!

NIA: uhhh, do they know where i am? did u tell them anything else???

ANNA: they don't...I swear... they even took my phone to check the history!!!... but i deleted our last chats tho!!! HA! :O

NIA: nice job!!! :) does anyone else know?

ANNA: NO!... but seriously, r u OK?

NIA: yeah... it's a long story...i'll tell u later, but i'm good. i mean, i need a shower and to change my underwear and sleep, but i'm totally fine.

ANNA: LOL! R u on your phone? I thought u were all paranoid??? they'll track it, Nia! then i'll get busted too!!! I wanna help u, but this is getting crazy!!!

NIA: OK. Don't worry. I'll cover for u later... but PLEASE erase this convo! I gotta go. Talk to u later! THNX for everything! DO NOT let them break u!!! Be strong!;)

ANNA: OK good luck!!!

"Totally fine?" I was far from totally fine! Why did I write that?

I swiped my phone back to screensaver, glanced around the cafe, and met the eyes of the barista. I didn't trust him. One phone call to the police and I was done. They could search my name, or phone, and my parents would be on the next plane to Budapest.

Done.

Game Over.

I couldn't let that happen. I had to leave. Yet as I packed up my stuff, I recognized that I didn't have anywhere to go.

My mind went to the only person I knew and trusted in this city: Kurt. In stupid desperation, I swiped my iPhone and searched for the number of hotels in Budapest: 2,159! I narrowed it down to the city center: 492 hotels.

Hopeless.

I shut off my phone.

Avoiding eye contact with the barista guy, I picked up my bag and left. Even though Anna and Dumas had helped remind me of my mission, I got stuck on how I could find Kurt. I walked up and down the pedestrian streets downtown, hoping against all odds to randomly run into the old guy. I ended up in a nice big bookstore, scanning through the English section. On one hand, I was picturing how bored my classmates back in Sofia probably were, but part of me wished I could talk to my friends, and have lunch with Anna in our usual spot.

At around eleven a.m. I settled on the idea of finding a new reading spot and waiting till nine p.m. to go to the train station alone because, by that point, finding Kurt seemed impossible. On my way out of the bookstore the colorful photos on the cover of a travel book got my attention. I mean, I had a lot of time to kill. It was a book that focused on the Danube—the major river that bisected the city. I began skimming through pictures of the famous river, recalling how I had desperately run up to its edge just a few hours earlier. And that's when it hit me: the

Danube River! Kurt had mentioned it more than once, called it lovely, and connected it to fond memories with his wife!

In that moment I became convinced that he had to be staying at a hotel on the river. I rushed outside and went into the first cafe that had a 'free Wi-Fi' sign. I turned on my phone and searched exclusively for hotels on the Danube. After some mathematical and geographical calculations (For once, I thought, my teachers would be proud of me), I discovered that there were seventeen hotels that lined the river. By 12:45 I had sent all seventeen the same email under a false name:

Dear ----- Hotel,

My name is Sofia and I am searching for my great-grandfather, Kurt Chavez. He wandered off early this morning without getting his medication that I was supposed to give him. He has dementia and has this weird habit of checking into random hotels because he thinks he's on a business trip. Sadly, this has happened before, but I am extra worried today. If Kurt Chavez has checked into your hotel this morning, PLEASE contact me as soon as possible.

Sincerely,

Sofia Chavez

KURT

By 1 p.m. I was walking out of the hotel and into a taxicab. Ten minutes later, the taxi dropped me off in front of a flower shop on Kozma Street across from the cemetery. I bought twelve roses for Maria to represent how many years ago she'd passed away. It boggled my mind. *How had I gone on living without her for so long?*

Új köztemető, the Budapest Public Cemetery, was so enormous that when the guard saw me hobbling through the front gate, he had a young man go get a golf cart from around the corner and drive me to Maria's grave. He carted me half a kilometer or so, straight to her spot. The grass was already sprinkled with a few early fall leaves. I had to walk no more than ten meters. I asked the chauffeur to pick me up thirty minutes later and he nodded politely.

As usual, I sat down on the flat, limestone grave next to Maria's modest headstone, laid down my flowers, and spoke out loud as if she could hear me. I thanked her for her first smile, her first laugh, her first walk with me. I thanked her for marrying me and moving to California, for our daughter, for our love—for every memory, even the bad ones. Then, as was my tradition, I told her a story. She always loved hearing my stories, or so she said. First, I told her about my previous day because it was so eventful—my budget flight to Belgrade, my helping Nia on the train, talking to her, listening to her, and how her cowlick sparked memories. I imagined Maria smiling at my telling of it.

I then jumped back in time to the last conversation I had with Maria. I described the setting in the hospital, as if she wasn't there. I spoke not about the things I said—because she'd already heard them—but what I didn't say. That's the hard thing about knowing someone and loving someone and watching them die. There are all those words you wish you would've said, but didn't. Well, I told her right there at her gravesite. I spoke with my eyes closed and imagined her standing in front of me. I spoke for maybe twenty minutes straight. I won't say what I told her because some things are too private, too personal to share. When I got to the end, I cried unashamedly. As I sat there sobbing, I felt a sharp pain in my chest. I believed, for a few seconds, that I might die right then and there. It would have been the most poetic ending. I wouldn't have minded such an end at all—in fact, I would have welcomed it—but it wasn't meant to be.

I recovered and said a few words in Hungarian, mostly because she always laughed at my awful accent any time I attempted her language. And I desperately wanted her to laugh, to feel it resonate, to envision her glowing face, wherever she was. When the cart driver returned a few minutes later, I gazed at her headstone one last time, made a promise, and walked away.

NIA

For the next hour my eyes were glued to my iPhone screen. Within ten minutes I was getting messages in broken English that ranged from the brief ("No Kurt Chavez here. Sorry.") to the super long-winded (step-by-step instructions on how to inform the Hungarian authorities about a missing person). It was around 1:30 p.m. when I got the golden message:

> *"Dear Sofia: Mr Kurt Chavez checked into the Art'Otel early this morning. He is not answering his room phone at the moment. Please call us immediately and we will be happy to assist you. Kind Regards, Karina Kovacs."*

I immediately searched online and found Art'Otel on the map. It was just across the river, only one kilometer away!

As I stuffed *Monte Cristo* and my iPhone into my bag, it started ringing. I almost dropped it when I saw the word 'DAD' filling the bottom third of the screen. *Ahhhh!* I turned it off, threw it in my bag, ran outside and toward the river. If it was anything like the movies, and my parents already had the police searching for me, they could use my phone to track my location while it was online, for sure.

Crossing the bridge over the Danube, I considered dumping my phone into the river, but then came to my senses about a few things:

1) This was a very expensive phone,

2) I wasn't Jason Bourne, and

3) It couldn't be traced as long as the thing was shut off, *right*?

The receptionist at the Art'Otel seemed very concerned when I approached the front desk and identified myself as Sofia. The receptionist's name—Karina—was pinned to her blouse. She was the one who'd responded to my email, so she already knew my fabricated little story.

"Would you like me to call your great-grandfather's room, Sofia?"

"Yes, please," I said.

When she called me "Sofia" I had to stop myself from laughing. She called Kurt's room again, but there was no answer.

"I can wait in the lobby until he gets back," I said, feeling much better knowing I'd found Kurt's hotel and that he didn't really have dementia. "No problem."

"Are you sure he's okay?" she said, peering through the lobby windows like the outside world had become the arena in the Hunger Games. "I should call the police."

"No!" I said. "I mean, please don't. He would be so embarrassed."

Karina didn't look at me suspiciously. She seemed genuinely worried, as if she didn't want to be in any way connected to the loss (or death) of this senile American guest.

"Don't worry about it," I said. "He'll probably be back soon. Kurt always does this."

"Ahh, okay," she said, "You call your great-grandfather by his first name?"

"Sometimes," I said, and smiled. *Damn it, I had to be more careful.*

I went to the lobby couch and plopped down.

I didn't realize I had dozed off until Karina was gently patting my knee.

"Are you okay, Sofia?"

I was confused at first. *Who is this? Why is she calling me Sofia? Where am I?* It only took about three seconds to figure it all out.

"Yes, I'm fine."

"You must have fallen asleep for a few minutes," she said.

Her English was good—barely any accent.

"I guess I'm exhausted from searching for K—for my great-grandpa all morning."

"And your parents are... working?"

"Yes," I said. It wasn't a lie.

Unless they are out searching for me...

"If there's anything I can do to help, please let me know," Karina said.

"Thanks for being so nice," I said, and racked my brain. "Well, I'm not so worried about my great-grandpa getting hurt or wandering too far off. It's his medication—I mean, the medication that he hasn't taken yet—that's really the problem. As long as he makes it back here within an hour or so. I have his pills right here in my bag."

The lies were flowing now, so I decided to stop before I said something stupid, not that Karina suspected me of anything. In fact, it was quite the opposite.

"This is too bad," she said. "You must have not slept at all. Your great-grandfather must have left your house very early this morning."

"Yes," I said. "Very."

The receptionist's tone was so kind it gave me a twinge of guilt for lying so much.

"Have you called him?" Karina asked.

"No, he doesn't have a cell phone. He's really old school, ya' know."

It might have been too much American slang for Karina because she vaguely nodded then looked toward the window as if she were in deep thought.

"Do you have any idea where he might have gone?" she asked.

"No, but..." I said, "Maybe there's a clue in his hotel room?"

I must have sounded like a little girl playing detective with her friends at a sleepover. Karina winced at the idea at first, but seemed to be considering the alternative—a disheveled teenage girl sprawled across the lobby couch in a four-star hotel for who-knows-how long—because she asked me:

"You really need some sleep, don't you?"

"Well, I am tired," I said, "and starting to get more worried."

When I told the kind receptionist this, she and her loud heels promptly clicked back to her desk and returned with a white key card.

"Here, take this," Karina told me and winked. "Room number 24. Have some rest in your great-grandfather's room. I'm sure he'll be delighted to see you there, right?"

"Oh, he'll love it," I said with a smile.

Lying was becoming more and more natural to me.

KURT

Instead of taking the taxi directly back to my hotel, I asked the driver to drop me off on Vaci Street so I could walk by the old bakery. I imagined it might spark some good memories but my brief stroll had the opposite effect. Vaci Street was nothing like it used to be. Polished, re-designed, and trendy, I could barely recognize it. I managed to guess where the bakery was once located, but it bore no resemblance. Still I peeked through the window, hoping to get a glimpse of something interesting, at least a flashback of that wavy hair, but it was now a taco shop with one blonde guy inside cleaning the salsa-covered countertops.

I sat down on a bench because my feet ached and I was tired of standing up. The problem was that after ten minutes of sitting down I knew my decrepit bones would be tired of sitting, too. My body was no damned good anymore.

For the first time that afternoon, I wondered about Nia. Was she safe? Had she boarded another train to Berlin already? Would her parents find her? Would her foolish plan for revenge (or was it redemptive love?) work out? I knew the answer was most probably negative, but for some reason I didn't want to be so cynical. Nia was a true romantic, like Dumas, and there didn't seem to be too many of those around these days. I enjoyed Nia's spirit, her conviction, her determination. She'd given me a boost of adrenaline that I didn't think existed for me anymore. And it wasn't just about coming to her rescue with my cane. It was more personal than that. Nia's hair and cowlick weren't the only things that reminded me of Maria...

When I brought Maria back to America and we got married, our wedding night was unexpectedly strange. We made it to our honeymoon suite late that night and Maria told me that she was nervous.

I told her that was understandable, but soon realized that she was almost hyperventilating. She started whimpering and I was very confused. I asked her what was wrong.

It took her a while to find the words and build the courage to speak. She finally told me that when the Nazis occupied Budapest, they raided her family's home suspecting them of illegally hiding Jews. They weren't, but Maria's father cursed them for throwing furniture around and disrespecting his household. For this they took him outside and shot him.

This tragic story I knew already in less detail, but what I didn't know was that later the next day one Nazi soldier returned to Maria's home, beat her and raped her. When she told me this, I was both indignant and powerless. The damage had been done. I could do nothing but be the best husband to her that I could and help heal the emotional scars by loving her until the day I died. But I didn't get to do that, either.

Twelve years ago her doctor told us that she had breast cancer in its late stages. It pulled my heart down to the damned linoleum floor. But I promised her she would make it and I would help her fight it. Four months later she was dead. I was devastated and powerless again. I wanted to save her, to help her in all ways and in any way, but what could I do? Nothing.

Now, here was Nia. I did help her—but did I help her enough? I wasn't so enfeebled, even though I'd never been physically weaker since I reached the age of three. And she needed support and care, what with her neglectful parents who sounded like they were straight out of a Dickens novel. Should I have left her so abruptly at the train station? Should I have given her more advice? Contacted her parents and explained her poor choices? And what did that adorably honest line of hers at the train station mean, about being "partners"?

Sitting on that bench, I pondered my brief time with Nia for a few minutes until I stood up, hobbled in the direction of the Danube, and began to reason her away. It would be illogical—probably illegal—for an old man like me to accompany a female minor on a train to a foreign country. She had ditched school, stolen her parents' money, and lied repeatedly to avoid getting caught. I would be an accomplice—and a rather irresponsible geriatric one.

Better that she figure this all out on her own.

And then, of course, there was my own plan—the plan I had started considering months before my trip, one of the reasons I'd insisted on going alone, one of the reasons I'd packed so light. I didn't want any witnesses (especially a teenage one) or any other messy entanglements. My plan had become even more solidified when I'd stared down at Maria's grave that afternoon and made her a solemn promise:

That I'd go back to my hotel room.

Ingest far too many pills at one time.

And join Maria in the hereafter.

NIA

It was weird being in Kurt's hotel room by myself. I mean, he could have returned in five minutes or five hours, and I was intruding. Uninvited. *Would he be happy to see me or furious that I'd stalked him and invaded his privacy?*

I turned on the TV, but shut it off ten minutes later when I realized that I had no interest in the ten channels available, and that my patience for watching TV shows had been severely decreased due to YouTube.

I didn't want to use my phone because I didn't want to be tracked.

There was no choice but to keep reading *Monte Cristo*.

I sped through some of the tiresome, behind-the-scenes Paris deals that the Count was crafting. I mean, it was cool that the Count was disguised and fooling his adversaries, setting them up to ruin their lives through their own vices, but it dragged on a bit. I finally made it to a romantic scene when the Count is at the summer ball and sees Mercedes, his lost love. The Count, or Edmund Dantes, and Mercedes finally talked to each other in private, having an intimate moment almost twenty years after their engagement was ruined by his betrayal and imprisonment. Though she'd married and had a family in Paris, she still seemed interested in the Count—and suspected he was really Edmund Dantes. But he acted removed after having gone through his suffering. I put myself in his shoes as Mercedes asked:

> *"Do you live alone then?"*
>
> *"I do," said Monte Cristo.*
>
> *"You have no sister… no father?"*
>
> *"I have no one."*
>
> *"How can you live thus, with no one to attach you to life?"*
>
> *"It's not my fault, madame… I loved a young girl… I thought she loved me well enough to wait for me… When I returned she was married… perhaps my heart was weaker than that of others, and in consequence I suffered more than they would have done in my place. That's all."*

I pictured Alex.

I thought of Victoria.

I felt alone and became certain that continuing with Kurt was the only way.

KURT

When the taxi dropped me off at the hotel, a wave of melancholia swept through me. The lobby was eerily empty. My legs became wobbly in the elevator on the way up. When I made it to my hotel room door I paused and couldn't help but reflect: *That's the last time I'll see the Danube, use my feet to walk through this city—any city. No continental breakfast tomorrow. No tomorrow, for God's sake!*

Despite my regrets, it had become increasingly difficult to simply walk, to enjoy food, to get out of bed in the morning. Yes, I was resolved to end my life in the Art'Otel and make Budapest my final resting place. It was my promise to Maria.

When I opened the door and saw Nia sleeping on the mini couch with a book resting on her chest, I couldn't wrap my mind around it. I blurted out "What the hell?" at high volume.

"Surprise," she said, sitting up blurry-eyed.

"Surprise my foot! What in tarnation?"

Nia giggled at me—the *nerve*.

"Did you just say 'What in *tar-nation*?'" she asked.

"Oh, button your lip. I'm old!" I yelled, "And you have no business being here!"

"Well, I'm sorry, but I do have some business here."

"What's that?"

"Maybe you should sit down," she said as if she were my damned counselor.

Aggravated and flustered, I reluctantly took a seat.

Nia continued, "That man from the train, the rapist guy, is dead—I mean, you killed him."

I had no immediate response. I hadn't expected to hear that news. I truly thought I had only knocked the bastard out. But I have to admit that I didn't feel particularly bad about him being dead.

"Well, I'll be damned," I said and stared blankly at the hardwood floor.

"Don't feel bad, Kurt, remember you saved me."

She had misinterpreted my response as remorse.

"I suppose so," I said.

"And that's the other thing," Nia added excitedly. "I've been looking for you all day. I'm here to ask you to travel to Berlin with me. I feel like I can't do it without you, Kurt. I feel safer with you, and you can help me execute my *Monte Cristo* plan too."

Her smile was so hopeful—her voice annoyingly enthusiastic. I didn't know what to say. *She'd looked all day—for me?*

"The answer is no, Nia," I said.

"Why not?" Her voice cracked.

"I have plans too," I said.

"What are they?"

She seemed to be on the verge of tears.

I paused.

I'm going to kill myself tonight...Could I say it out loud? Could I even do it, for God's sake?

Now I was the one holding back tears.

"What can an old fart like me do to help you, anyway?"

"You already have helped and... I don't know."

"Exactly, you don't know what the heck you're talking about, Nia."

She hesitated. Her eyes watered. Nia took a moment to refocus.

"But you're like family to me now," she said. "The only family I have."

This word—family—hit me unexpectedly. It meant that neglected Nia, unloved and troubled Nia, had bonded with me enough to fill the void of her absent family in only twelve hours.

Appalling, the state of family today.

But that was real love she felt—familial love. The only family I had left was my daughter, but she had drifted further and further away from me in her adulthood. She had her own life, a husband, her own grown child, now. I felt alone too—like Nia, alone in the world without bonds of real love. We shared the same kind of pain. It's what made me think of her during the day and what made my mind try to reason her away, out of fear. But I've always believed that love is greater than fear. The Greeks called it *storge*—the caring that one has between children and parents. Unconditional empathy. We needed more of that in the world, there is no doubt. Now Nia was reaching out, asking for a hand. And there I was ready to kill myself—the most selfish way to end my earthly suffering.

Nia's face angled down at her shoes. I glanced at my toiletry bag on the end table, filled with all my medication. I took a seat on the edge of the bed and noticed her teary cheeks.

"What do you want me to do, Nia?"

"I want you to come to Berlin with me."

"On the train?"

"Yes," she asserted.

I gazed down at my wrinkled, reptilian hands. They were arthritic, but still alive. Yes, alive, and what was the purpose of living? *To embrace unexpected twists on the journey!*

This made me feel young again—maybe seventy-nine or eighty.

"When does it leave?" I asked.

"In five hours."

Nia grinned, extended her hand, and I shook it to seal the deal the old fashioned way. It may sound crazy or irrational, but that very craziness was part of why I agreed to go with her.

NIA

I took a long nap in Kurt's room while he stayed awake and read some *Monte Cristo*. At around seven p.m., after I freshened up a bit in the loo, we grabbed our small travel bags and took the elevator down to find somewhere to eat dinner near the hotel. On the way past the front desk, I dropped my key card and a note with the new receptionist, not Karina. This makeup heavy receptionist peered at the envelope with "NIA" written on it and then back at me.

"Who is for?" she asked.

"My mom or dad might come by looking for us," I said. "If they ask about me or my grandpa, please give them this note," I said.

"Okay... but you have no phone?"

"It's dead," I said and turned to meet Kurt at the front door.

We went to the right, just outside the Art'Otel, and there it was. As if Kurt's willingness to accompany me to Berlin wasn't inspiration enough, what was the name of the first restaurant we saw? *Café Dumas!* It was a sign, right there in red neon light. Of course, Alexander Dumas was the author of *The Count of Monte Cristo*. It reaffirmed that my mission was not in vain. *It was all going to work!*

The inside of Cafe Dumas was dark and lacked atmosphere. Only one other table was occupied, by a Hungarian couple. Our dinner conversation was a bit slow and awkward at first, maybe because in our last talk, I had proclaimed my needy bond to Kurt and he'd agreed to travel with a runaway teen. On top of that, we were pretty much strangers separated by seventy-four years who had met each other less than twenty-four hours before.

"Was Budapest this cool way back when you first came here?"

"It was better," Kurt said.

"Why? How?"

"Not as many advertisements. Not as much consumerism," he said. "People appreciated the little things more."

"Why do old people always say how much better it was back in the old days?"

"Is that what your grandpa says?" Kurt asked.

"My Bulgarian grandpa hated communism while it was around, then strangely loved it when it was gone." I said. "It doesn't make any sense."

"And your American grandpa?"

"I never knew him. He died when I was two."

Kurt frowned.

He was really beginning to seem like the American grandpa that I never had.

The waiter appeared. Kurt ordered the chicken and potatoes. I ordered pasta carbonara. When I turned from the waiter back to Kurt, his eyes were all lit up.

"What's up, Kurt? Are you okay?

"Yes," he said. "I just realized that I lied to you."

My heart sunk from the unexpected disappointment.

"Lied about what?"

"Remember when you asked if I ever killed someone and I told you the story about shooting the young German during the war?"

"How could I forget?"

"Well, I just remembered that I killed a priest too," Kurt said. "Unintentionally, of course."

I was relieved that Kurt's lie wasn't directly about me or our trip, but how many people had this guy killed?

"Seriously? How?"

Kurt took a long sip of water as if he needed some fuel to tell the story.

"About thirty years ago I invited a friend, Mike, over to my house for dinner, and Mike brought a priest. The priest was a chubby, rosy-cheeked old guy who'd just returned from a stint in Assisi, Italy. He raved about Italian food, so I took it as a personal challenge to make him some great pasta that night. I had learned one key chef's rule from my Italian friend before he got his head blown off in Jesberg: Cook with a heavy hand. So when I added salt, cream, butter, oil, and bacon, I did so with reckless abandon. The result was one of the best pastas I'd ever made! We all blathered about it during the meal, and the priest stuffed himself as he repeatedly confirmed its authentic, excellent quality. The problem was that I didn't know this priest had high blood pressure, high cholesterol, *and* diabetes! It wasn't until after dinner that he mentioned he needed to take his medication and Mike reminded him that his pills were back at his place. Caution to the wind, that chubby old priest stayed and drank red wine in my living room into the wee hours. When they got up to go, I walked them to my front porch. That's when the priest gasped in pain, grabbed his chest, and fell down."

"He had a heart attack?"

"Yes, indeed," Kurt said. "He died right there on my lawn. We didn't know what the heck to do and the paramedics took too long to get there."

"Come on, Kurt," I said. "You didn't really kill that priest."

"Sure I did," he said.

"But he was the one who forgot to take his pills," I reasoned. "And he should not have eaten so much or drank wine all night."

"Would-a, could-a, should-a," he quipped.

"Come on, it was a combination of factors, Kurt."

"Isn't everything?"

When my pasta carbonara arrived, I approached it with caution. Kurt didn't even notice my timid eating style. He was too involved with his chicken. He seemed so calm and unaffected. But I couldn't help thinking about the fact that the attempted rapist guy was dead, my parents were trying to contact me all day, Anna was being interrogated, and there was a rumor I'd been kidnapped!

Of course, I wasn't going to tell Kurt any of this.

"So that makes it three, huh," I said.

"Three what?"

"Three people you've killed."

"Well," Kurt said. "I suppose so."

KURT

At dinner, my mind fought with my heart over the fact that I was still alive and sitting across from an eighth grade girl. *And* I had killed three people in my lifetime. That was nothing to be proud of. Lost in my internal struggle at first, I eventually tuned-in to my dinner guest as she began to open up about her family.

"My mom moved to Bulgaria when she was twenty-four," Nia said, "I was only three."

"So your mom spoke to you in English?" I asked.

"Yeah, most of the time. She can speak a little Bulgarian, but not very well. I can tell when she's really mad at my dad because she yells at him entirely in English to piss him off."

"Is that why your English is so good? You don't really have an accent."

"I guess so," she said. "There's also the school I go to—the American International School. There's maybe 50% Bulgarians there, but all the teachers are from the US, UK, or Canada, so I speak English all the time—sometimes more than Bulgarian even though I've lived in Sofia almost all my life."

"Do you like your school?" I asked.

"Now *that* is a grandpa question, for sure."

"Seriously."

"You mean, like my classes and my grades?" Nia said.

"No, I mean do you like the place, your classmates?"

"Well, it's kind of a ridiculous place. It's in the middle of one of the poorest countries in Europe which has a really bad education system, but it's a super nice new campus that's like a bubble of fancy imported American education."

"What's the tuition?"

"30,000 euros per year."

"Holy cow," I said. "And what are the other students like?"

"Weird," she said. "I mean, there's kids from all over the world—India, Brazil, Japan, Canada, the UK, Israel. Some of their parents work in embassies or for big companies. And then there's the Bulgarians, usually filthy rich and more concerned about the price of their shoes than anything else."

"And how do you fit in?"

"Pretty well, because I'm Bulgarian and American. But the problem is that there's no one else like me there—except my friend Anna. I can speak both languages fluently, but it's like I can't be both. I have to choose one or the other: either hangout with the Bulgarians or with the Americans. There's judgment either way, based on which one I choose. It's like I'm not American enough for the Americans, and not Bulgarian enough for the Bulgarians!"

"So what do you chose?"

"I don't. I try to be myself."

"Smarter than I was at your age," I confessed.

"You had the same problem?" Nia asked.

"Yes, I did. My mom was a white American and my dad was Mexican-American—Raul Chavez. I grew up speaking both languages. Back in my day, you not only had to choose, you had to choose to be white! At least that's what I thought. Choosing to be Mexican in America back then was like asking to be labeled a criminal and targeted by the police. It was a racist place and still is, but in different ways. My dad pretty much told me to be "American" if I wanted to succeed. So I learned to read and write English to the best of my ability, stopped speaking Spanish, and joined the Army to prove my patriotism."

"Did it work?"

"In some ways, yes," I said. "But it took me a lot longer to get to where you are now with your identity—to realize that I was both Mexican and white; that I didn't have to choose; that I should just be true to myself."

"Why do you say 'white'? What was your mom?" Nia asked, genuinely perplexed.

"Oh, her family was mostly German, but when you live in America, that eventually just becomes 'white.'"

"That's weird."

"Yeah, it is," I said.

"I thought Americans were all super-sensitive about racism," she said, "but it seems like it's even a bigger problem there."

"Yeah, it does."

"I mean, you'd think that America—with Martin Luther King and its history—would have it figured out by now."

"Yep."

"But, apparently not," she said. "Maybe I'll run for president one day."

"You've got my vote," I said, and it was the damned truth.

By the end of the dinner, I was glad that Nia had saved my life—though she was still oblivious to the fact that she had.

NIA

There were a few taxis waiting right outside the Art'Otel, so Kurt and I walked the half a block back from the restaurant to get our cab to the train station. Even though the old guy was as slow as syrup, I felt better with him by my side, like we were a team—a very *slow* team.

But something else was bugging me. A few times since texting with Anna, I worried about my iPhone being tracked. Whether my parents still believed I'd been kidnapped (something that actually happened to rich kids in Bulgaria) or had figured out by now that I ran away, they had definitely informed the police already and who knew what else. It made me wonder what other measures my parents were taking to find me.

Kurt ducked into the Mercedes taxi and I stood waiting for his frail body to get settled. I scanned the road along the river and noticed the driver of a sleek, black Passat eyeing me. He immediately got out of his car as if he recognized me. *Creepy.* I dove into the taxi and closed the door without wasting another second. Through the window I saw the Passat guy, dressed in a dark suit with no tie, quickly approaching us. "Let's go!" I said to the taxi driver. The man could have been any random guy with a shiny Passat entering the Art'Otel, but I assumed the worst. *CIA? Interpol? Undercover detective?* Then he appeared right outside my door and knocked on the window!

"Go!" I yelled at our driver, and we sped off.

I watched through the back window as the Passat guy ran to his car, made a U-turn, and followed us.

"What's the rush?" Kurt said. "And who the heck was that?"

"I don't know," I said.

"Then why are you acting so spooked?" he said.

"I'm guessing it's a private investigator looking for me," I said. "My parents must know."

"Know what?"

"My dad called me this morning and I didn't answer," I said. "But I was online for at least an hour so they might have tracked my phone's location."

"Oh, dear," Kurt said, "They can do that with phones now?"

It was kind of funny and beyond old school, but it was no time for laughter.

"Yes!" I said.

Kurt started to turn his head and shift his body around to spot the car following us, but he groaned in pain and grabbed his neck.

"Goddammit," he said, facing forward again.

"Are you alright?" I asked.

"Yeah," he said. "Is that guy still following you?

"Us," I corrected.

"Indeed."

"Yes, he is!"

The Passat was right behind us. We neared a big intersection with a light that had just turned red. I was afraid that if we were stopped so close to each other, the Passat guy might get out of his car and try to pull me out of the taxi. *Game over.* We were already slowing to a full stop at the front of the intersection. I pulled out 100 euros from my bag, showed it to the driver, and asked if he would gas it and shoot the light if the man behind us got out of his car. The taxi driver glanced at the bill—not at me—and didn't respond.

Both of us were at a complete stop now. I turned around and saw the Passat driver's side door open. I twisted back to our driver and said "Go now!" Without hesitation, he floored it and we zipped through the intersection. It wasn't smooth like in the movies, but it worked. Kurt yelled "Goddammit!" as we screeched away, leaving the Passat behind us. Our cab driver, perhaps with his adrenaline flowing, drove dangerously fast through the city streets for a few more minutes. I looked back through the window and couldn't spot the Passat anywhere.

"For God's sake!" said Kurt.

"Okay, slow down," I told the driver. "You don't have to drive so crazy."

He replied in his bad English, "Crazy? You the crazy!"

Kurt had let out a few old man expletives during our brief chase sequence, so when it was all over I patted him on his wrinkly hand.

"I'm sorry, Kurt," I said. "I promise the rest of the trip to Berlin won't be so fast and furious."

Surprisingly, he said: "This kind of excitement sure beats being dead."

His joke struck me as morbid, but I laughed anyway. And, on second thought, Kurt didn't look worried at all. He was smiling. In fact, it seemed like he was having fun!

By the time we made it to the train station, I was mildly freaking out. If the Passat guy private detective, or whoever it was, kept searching for me, wouldn't the train station be too risky?

I turned to Kurt. "What if the Hungarian police or Interpol are searching for me? Would they connect us to the attempted rapist guy's death?"

He said nothing so I kept up the questions. "What would happen if we got caught? Would they put me in jail? And what about you? Are you too old to go to prison?"

I was definitely too young to go to prison!

KURT

Nia was a bit paranoid as we entered the Budapest central train station. Perhaps she felt all the consequences of running away from home, stealing and deception catching up to her. She kept asking a bunch of hypothetical questions.

"Nia, remember what I said about worrying too much?"

"No," she said.

"Namely, it's a waste of time."

To ease her mind, I told her that I'd buy the train tickets to Berlin. If they were searching for suspects in the murder of the guy I had accidentally killed, I probably wouldn't be on their list. Even if I was, I wouldn't care if I got caught. If there were people looking for her, well, they could be anywhere—back at the hotel, the airport, the rest of the city. From the unsatisfied expression on Nia's face, she clearly didn't understand (or didn't want to accept) my reasoning. I stood in the short line, no more that twenty feet away from her, and paid in cash—part of the money I'd stashed away for my own burial.

I didn't want to explain to Nia that, prior to seeing her surprise appearance in my room, my evening plans were to be dead already. Being that I was alive and well, with a dose of natural adrenaline coursing through me, I had a new lease on life. My joints ached a little bit less than usual. My mind felt a little bit sharper. When I handed Nia her ticket and smiled, she gave me a curious stare.

"Why are you being so weird?"

"Weird?" I said.

"So relaxed," she clarified.

"We're going to Berlin. I've heard it's a great city."

"That's exactly what I'm talking about, Mr. Casual," she said. "There might be people here looking for us—the police! The Embassy and CIA agents are connected to my school. They could be searching for me too."

"So they catch you," I said. "Big deal. You're going to get caught sometime."

Nia seemed to be pondering whether my statement was a joke, or not.

"Not before I get to Berlin," she said.

"Maybe, maybe not," I said. "Is that really all that important Nia, getting to Berlin?"

"What?!" she exploded. "It's the only thing that's important to me right now!"

Reminded that my companion was an irrational teen driven by her raging hormones, I switched gears.

"Nia, all I'm saying is that there's a lot that we don't know right now. Why worry if that worry is based on speculation and imagination?" I said. "That guy in the Passat might have mistaken you for someone else. Maybe your iPhone wasn't tracked. Maybe nobody in the world has a clue where you are right now except Yours Truly."

Nia paused, surveyed the scene at the old-fashioned train station and saw nothing out of the ordinary. Because of Nia's keen mind and sense of purpose, I sometimes forgot she was only a kid. But in that moment, unsure and fearful, she looked about five years old—until the sudden shift.

"Maybe," she said, and then her eyes brightened. "You're right. No worries."

"Did something change?" I asked.

"I almost forgot about the note."

"What note?"

"The note I left at the hotel front desk."

"What does it say?" I asked.

"It says that I'm not kidnapped, and that we're going to the Budapest airport tonight."

"But we're not anywhere near the airport," I said dumbly.

"Exactly," she said.

Clever girl.

PART III: On to Berlin

NIA

It was hard to believe that we'd arrived at this train station early that same morning—it all seemed so long ago. After Kurt's old man advice and remembering my diversionary note, I stopped suspecting that *every* fairly athletic, decently dressed man in the station was an undercover agent pursuing me.

Kurt and I boarded the train, and found our cabin—no problem. It was a private sleeper with two bunk beds. Part of me liked that we could lock the door and no one could barge into our space, but the other part of me felt kind of awkward knowing I was going to sleep in the same small space as Kurt. *Would he snore? Hang out in his boxers? Fart? Wet the bed—or worse, wear old man diapers?* I didn't want to find out any of these details. I picked the top bunk figuring it would be impossible, or at least extremely difficult, for grandpa Kurt to get up or down from there. He sat on the lower bunk, took off his shoes, laid down, made a few arthritic moans and said "Dadgummit!"

I laughed.

He sounded annoyed with me, but his old man-ism's were hilarious.

Who says dadgummit and tarnation?

"What's wrong?" I asked.

"I'm a twit. I forgot to check out of the hotel," he said as he held out the hotel key card for me to see.

"It's okay," I told him, "I gave them my key... We had no time anyway."

"Yeah, I paid when I checked in, but I still have this damn key," Kurt said. "I hope they don't bust me for this."

A full second passed before we both laughed out loud.

The train whistle blew.

I stared down at the adjacent tracks through the dark window as our train crept out of Budapest and into the night. Two minutes later Kurt was snoring like an elderly bear.

I went back to reading *The Count of Monte Cristo*. I was in the last chapters when the Count is in the thick of exacting his revenge. He'd gotten to Mondego and Villefort, and Danglars was next. But two things happened that I didn't expect. I thought the Count would forgive Mercedes and their love would be renewed, but no. The Count felt betrayed and was convinced that Mercedes had a choice and that she had betrayed him. *Game over*. No more love lost there. And then the Count has this moment when he questions his whole mission to get vengeance.

Had he gone too far?

Was I going too far?

It made me realize that I didn't have much of a plan for Berlin. So I put down the book, tied my hair in a ponytail and came up with one: I would get a room at the Radisson (Kurt would help me with this since I was under eighteen). I'd send Alex a text letting him know that I was coincidentally in Berlin and alone in my hotel room. Right before he came to visit me, I'd send Victoria a message to come to my room too. Before opening the door for her, I'd strip down to only my bra and underwear and Alex would be caught inside my room! Just seeing Alex with me half-dressed would humiliate Victoria, and then Alex would have to choose whom he preferred.

But, like the Count and Mercedes, would I even want to be with Alex if he chose me? After all, it was his 'free will' to leave me and jump into the arms of Victoria so quickly. And what had they been up to over the past two days? I hadn't checked any of my social media feeds.

It might be risky to use my phone again, but maybe old-school Kurt was right—could phones be so easily traced? I pulled out my phone, turned it on, and lowered the volume so I wouldn't wake up Kurt. My screen lit up, buzzed and vibrated with so many updates it was shocking. My mom and dad had called at least ten times each. There were a bunch of unfamiliar numbers too—the police? —my school? I connected to the train's free Wi-Fi. My social media feeds were on fire with messages and notifications: 39 and 136! I had to check.

Maybe part of me wanted to get caught before the showdown in Berlin. Maybe part of me knew I had taken this thing too far already.

Staring at my screen, I felt a wave of concern from a bunch of people I thought had very little interest in me—especially my parents. But my plan to check all my posts and messages was stopped dead in its tracks when I saw the news headline posted on my feed:

Bulgarian Teen Kidnapped by Killer, Search is on!

My heart almost stopped. Maybe because the breath and life had been knocked out of me by the words KIDNAPPED, KILLER and SEARCH in news print. Suddenly, I was like a contestant in *The Hunger Games*. Katniss Everdeen. Only I didn't have to kill anyone or be killed. I imagined police sirens, helicopters, bright searchlights, and me trying to outrun them all. For some dumb reason, I saw it as a challenge. *Mission Impossible* for an eighth grader. I simply had to make it to Berlin without getting caught, complete my mission and then deal with the consequences from there. I braced myself and read the article:

> *A Bulgarian teenager has been kidnapped*
> *by an English-speaking man who has yet to*
> *be identified but is assumed to be armed and*
> *dangerous. The fourteen-year-old was*
> *abducted in downtown Sofia, Bulgaria on*

Thursday morning and transported by train to Belgrade, Serbia, then to Budapest, Hungary, where the kidnapper checked into a hotel room with the victim. It is believed that the kidnapper killed a man on the train en route to Budapest, presumably in an effort to maintain possession of the teenage girl. It is believed that the kidnapper and murder suspect is involved in a large sex trafficking ring that targets young girls.

Thanks to a tracking device installed by Apple, the teenager's iPhone was traced to Budapest the morning after her parents alerted the authorities that she was missing late on Thursday night. On Friday evening a private investigator identified the kidnapped girl as the suspect forced her into a taxi along the Danube, but lost her in a high-speed chase. It is unknown whether the kidnapper is working alone or is part of a larger network. The Hungarian police returned to the Budapest hotel where the girl and her abductor stayed and are currently working on leads.

The teenage girl is said to have skipped school Thursday morning and was abducted sometime soon after. Her parents, both successful corporate executives, believe that the kidnappers expect to be paid ransom money, but have yet to contact them. Local reports in Budapest said the kidnapper and the teen were pretending to be grandfather and granddaughter. The identity of the kidnapper has not yet been discovered, but he is currently wanted for kidnapping and first degree murder. It is not clear if the suspect and girl are in Hungary or have moved on to a neighboring country. If you have any information regarding this case or can identify the missing teen (see pictured below), please email ---- or call +088 --------.

My seventh grade class photo stared back at me in full color on the ten by six centimeter screen! Crazy is a word that didn't do my situation justice. I had to force myself to inhale and exhale to prevent a panic attack. It was way more serious than even I had imagined. And the stuff they made up! Kidnapper? Murder? Abduction? Sex trafficking? Ransom money? Most of it was totally wrong! Did they even read my note at the hotel? And my phone, my stupid phone! I turned off the Wi-Fi and the phone, shoved it back in my bag, and vowed to myself to keep it off until I was at the Radisson.

KURT

I felt a small hand on my shoulder, shaking me back and forth, whispering urgently for me to get up. It took me awhile to come to and realize where I was—on a train to Berlin. It seemed incredible that I was still alive and it wasn't all a dream. Yes, my bones and joints ached for God's sake. At first, I didn't even recognize Nia—my short-term memory getting progressively worse with age. When my blurry eyes finally managed to pull focus, I could see that she was terrified.

"What the—

"It's official. You're wanted for murder and kidnapping," she said bluntly.

"Are you pulling my leg, Nia?"

She told me that she would read me the news article word for word aloud, but she'd just turned off her phone because it had been tracked back in Budapest and she didn't want to be located again. Nia told me all of the highlights of the news article and I was, well, shocked. The only difference between her and my reactions was that I was certain that all the mularkey would be cleared up in due time and there wasn't all that much to worry about.

"For God's sake, they make me sound dangerous—and young!" I said.

"The bigger the threat, the better the news story, right?"

"Well, Nia," I said, "Obviously we need to turn ourselves in before this gets any more ridiculous."

"Agreed," Nia said with curious conviction. "Tomorrow night. We turn ourselves in tomorrow night."

I explained to Nia that it had all gone too far. That her parents were suffering. That one or both of us could get hurt. That her plan to get back at the boy she loved and his new girl was not worth it. I thanked her for spicing up my life with this dramatic and unexpected twist, but I told her that it was over.

"To hell with this Berlin business," I said.

"No, it is not *Game Over*," Nia said.

"Nia, it's not a game."

"Do you really trust the police, Kurt? Do you trust they'll do the right thing?"

"Yes, I assume they will," I said.

"Think about *Monte Cristo*, I mean Edmund Dantes," Nia said. "He got screwed over by the law. He was thrown in jail for doing nothing. And when he escaped, he knew that the only way he'd get justice was by doing it his way, not going to the police or the courts. You know why?— Because they're corrupt!"

"Dumas wrote fiction, you know."

"But there is truth in it, otherwise everybody wouldn't read it and call it a classic, right?"

"True, but this is silly, Nia."

"Do you think the police are corrupt or not?"

"I assume some are, but most are not," I said.

"You've obviously never been to Bulgaria," she said. "And how do you know we—correction, you—will not be the one to get screwed over and end up in jail?"

"I don't know," I said, trying to gather my wits. "Dumas was making a point that legal justice is not always justice, but he also makes a point that the Count had gone too far in his plan, leaving too much death and suffering in his wake, and in the end—"

"Spoiler alert," she blurted out, "I still haven't finished the book!"

I sensed that I wasn't getting through to her, that years of bad parenting had made Nia somewhat of a lost cause. And for some reason I was reminded that I was miraculously still alive. For God's sake, I could've died next to a big tree in Jesberg in 1945—or killed myself earlier that evening in my hotel room! And there Nia stood, a face of hope on the verge of deflation.

So I gave in to her whim, again.

"But I'm an old fart," I said. "What do I care about any of this anyways? Honestly, who gives a rat's ass if I'm thrown in prison? It'll give me a chance to read those

Dostoyevsky novels I've been putting off. I have nothing to lose, I suppose."

With my last words, Nia's eyes squinted in confusion. It was as if I could hear her thinking out loud: *Nothing to lose? Do you have a death wish old man? What about me—your fake grandchild—you don't want to lose me, right?'* But she didn't say anything for a few long seconds. The sound of steel wheels on steel track was surprisingly faint. We were gliding through the darkness toward Berlin. Nia gave me a smirk and broke the silence. "So does that mean you're still in?

"In deep fecal matter?"

"No, *in* for keeping this mission going till tomorrow night? I need your help."

Against my better judgment, I nodded. It was as if my mind wouldn't allow me to say the word "yes" out loud, but my heart nodded for Nia's sake. I was always a sucker in this department. Nia let out a shrill squeal of excitement and smiled.

"You promise?" she said, sounding painfully young.

"I promise," I said.

"Looks like the romanticism of Dumas is still alive," she said.

"Sure, but here's some realism for you," I said. "I've got to pee like a racehorse."

NIA

The train had come to a full stop. When Kurt returned from the bathroom, he had the most concerned expression that I'd seen yet. He closed the door to our sleeper cabin and said:

"Nia, remember the deep feces I mentioned? Well, it's upon us."

"What's going on?"

"German border agents just got on this train and are approaching us, checking passports."

Oh, my God. If these German officers had any idea about us—and why not with the news headline and the dumb use of my phone—we would soon be cornered and caught. I remembered how the news article said that they didn't know Kurt's identity, but they knew all about me. I was the one who needed to hide.

"I'm going to hide in the bathroom," I told Kurt.

"The border patrol is coming right now!" he said. "It's not safe."

"I have to," I said. "I've made it this far and I'm not giving up."

"Pardon me, Nia, but you might be confusing bravery with foolishness.'

"Maybe," I said, "but will you at least play along for a little longer?"

Kurt scowled at me before he unveiled a smirk.

I told him to pretend like he spoke Spanish only. I told him to do the Catholic sign of the cross and act as Mexican as he could, just to throw them off the whole English-speaking suspect thing. I advised him to point to his last name, Chavez, in his passport and repeat the word Mexican a lot.

"That's ridiculous," he said. "It's not gonna work."

"It's gonna work," I said. "I'll be back soon."

Kurt took my hand in both of his wrinkly, soft hands and said, "Be careful, Nia."

His eyes were watery. I could see that he cared about me like one of his own grandchildren and—at that moment—I really felt like I was his grandkid.

I tried my best to calmly walk to the far end of the train. Luckily, the border guards weren't in the aisle and I didn't pass by anyone on the way to the WC. Once inside I closed and locked the door. The hard plastic flooring reeked of dried piss. *What would happen if they knocked? Would they wait or barge in?* They would probably have a train official open it up to check. It would be pretty suspicious to have a locked bathroom door and nobody inside. I noticed a small plastic cabinet next to the sink. It was locked but I managed to jerk it open without trying too hard. There was one plastic wrapped package of toilet paper inside and it smelled of stagnant water and urine. It looked impossibly small, even for a contortionist, but it was my only hope.

I unlocked the main bathroom door and eased into the tiny cabinet, butt first. I grabbed my feet and struggled to pull them inside. With my knees practically in my mouth and my spine smashed against a plastic wall, I felt a small puddle of water—I hoped it was water—soak into the butt of my pants. Disgusting. It could've been anything, and the stench didn't ease my mind. I almost forgot to close the cabinet doors from the inside but when I did, they didn't stay shut. I'd broken the cheap plastic lock when I forced it open!

I could hear the voices of the German officers as they got closer and imagined I was a Jew, hiding from Nazis during World War II. I ducked my head down and grabbed the hair tie off my ponytail. I forced my left hand free, closed the cabinet doors from the inside, tied the inner handle brackets tight with my hair tie, and waited in the dark.

Those few minutes felt like hours, but then there was a knock at the door and two German voices. Scary voices. I could have sworn I heard *Judenschwein*, but it was probably my movie-fueled imagination. Someone opened the bathroom door. Their boots sounded heavy and squeaked creepily. I tried my best not to breathe. One of them said *"Keiner"* and they closed the door and walked away. *Keiner?* It was definitely not the time to check Google translate.

Ten minutes later the train started moving again. I waited another ten minutes before daring to crawl from out of my cramped hiding spot. The whole time I wondered if my advice to Kurt had worked.

KURT

I have to admit it was good fun lying to those German border guards. It was an Academy Award-winning performance that only they got to witness. After showing them my passport and pointing to my last name, as Nia instructed, they asked a few questions.

"Are you traveling alone?" one officer asked.

"Me llamo Chavez. No hablo Ingles bien." I said, doing my best to play dumb.

"Have you seen anything suspicious?"

"No comprendo, amigos." I said and thought: *Why did Germans always speak such damn good English?*

"Mister, have you seen any... foreigners?"

"No foreigners. No puedo comprender. Gracias," I said, in my good-for-nothing-Spanish.

"Er ist zu alt," the other officer said.

I don't speak German, but when they abruptly exited I could tell they'd dismissed me as a senile old Mexican man. Maybe I should have been an actor? My Spanish was no good, but they didn't seem to know that and I was able to mix some Spanish with a few English words spoken in a decent accent. It was enjoyable pulling one over on two German officers. It was a kind of slapstick retribution.

After all, a number of Germans killed some of my young buddies long, long ago.

However, my acting pride soon faded when the officers left and I pondered the possibility of Nia being caught. Of course, it wouldn't be the end of the world for her, but I was now her partner in crime. I'd pledged my allegiance. At that point I knew I was doing the exact wrong thing, on the side of an ill-planned, borderline criminal teenage escapade. I was nearly ninety years old, had been a responsible teacher for almost thirty years and should have had an inkling of common sense left in me. But who out there hasn't known the right thing to do—the empirically correct decision to make—and then done the exact opposite? Sometimes the instinctive, less rational choice makes the most sense to us mammals, as paradoxical as it might sound.

So was I on that train only for Nia's sake, to support her adventure, her Monte Cristo inspired romantic mission? I'd like to offer a wholehearted "Yes," but I have to admit that I was selfishly enjoying the journey, able to live vicariously through Nia's young, courageous heart and clever mind.

Ten minutes passed, then twenty. The longer I waited in that solitary train cabin, the more I worried. Nia had been gone nearly thirty minutes. We were in Germany, now, in the homestretch. All she had to do was come back to the cabin in one piece, get some sleep, and we'd be in Berlin in the morning.

NIA

When I got back to the cabin, Kurt's big smile gave me a rush of warmth and confidence. We shared our brief fugitive stories and a few laughs, and then it was as if the old guy had popped some sleeping pills. He fell asleep like a log and was snoring again in no time. I changed into sweatpants, but it was hard to imagine falling asleep. Too much had happened, the circumstances were too extreme, and Kurt's snoring was too loud.

I stared at the ceiling, remembering the night I'd gotten into my first big argument with my mom. It was soon after the divorce. I'd told her I was going to Anna's house for dinner, but I was really walking around Sofia listening to Nirvana on my headphones, popping into shops and bookstores on my own. I loved the freedom. Unfortunately, one of my mom's friends saw me and sent her a message. When I got home around midnight my mother met me at the door. She stood there and looked at me as she never had before—as a criminal, an impostor, a burden. Her gaze alone created a distance that had never been there before. Then she slapped me, which didn't physically hurt but created even more distance. She called me a liar and told me to go to my room. I replied, "My room here, or at Dad's place?" She seemed to be on the verge of hitting me again, but held herself in check. At that moment she got a call, glanced at her screen, looked back at me, then answered it. It was a guy she was dating. I couldn't believe my mother. She'd chosen a guy she'd known for two weeks over her daughter in a crucial moment. I froze, waiting to see if she'd talk to me or ignore me completely. She got off the phone a few minutes later.

"Thanks for ruining my date tonight," she said.

"*I* ruined it?" I asked.

"Yes, because you lied to me. You lied, Nia!"

I could have left right then. Turned and walked to my dad's house, or gone straight to my room. Instead I said: "You lied, too."

She stood there, incredulous.

"You lied to me and dad when you were cheating on him," I asserted.

Her jaw dropped and eyes seemed to pierce right through me.

"Nia, do you think he was innocent? He was cheating on me first!" she yelled, then began to sob.

I didn't move an inch, sad and disappointed with both of them.

"You wouldn't understand," she added, before striding out to the balcony.

No, I didn't understand much of it. What I really couldn't comprehend was how my mother could only think about herself, her date and how others saw her, rather than making an effort to understand me—her daughter.

She felt betrayed, but so did I.

What I didn't recognize at the time was that I had lied to her first, and that her anger with me probably came from her concern about her teenaged daughter walking around the city at night; it was worry based on love. Something about this memory put my mind at ease.

I wasn't the only one who'd screwed up. They'd screwed up too.

Maybe it had to do with this realization, and maybe it had to do with the peaceful hum of the rails. But, miraculously, I conked out and slept soundly until morning.

Kurt's old man moaning and groaning woke me early. I rolled over in the narrow bunk bed and watched him doing simple yoga-like stretches as he gazed out the window at the green blur of trees whizzing by us. I didn't think he knew I was awake until he told me:

"Stretching is the key to fighting old age."

He said that most old people stop moving, stop stretching, and that's why their bodies slowly fall apart.

"Do you wanna get some coffee and breakfast?" I asked him.

"Sure," he said. "The cafe car should be open by now."

We left our tiny cabin ten minutes later.

I don't know if it was Kurt's influence, but I didn't worry much about the authorities catching us in the cafe car. I mean, what were the odds of one of the few people in there having read a Bulgarian news story about a kidnapped girl and then putting two and two together when they saw us? Not much. We sat down and a steward came over. Kurt waited until I had ordered a cappuccino to tell me that I was too young to be drinking coffee.

"You sound like my mom."

"Maybe you should listen to her," he said, taking a sip of his Americano. "Coffee isn't good for young bones."

"It isn't good for *bones*, period." I said. "How do adults not see the hypocrisy of telling a kid not to do something that they do everyday—like drinking coffee? My parents are freaking addicts."

"Good point, Nia."

"Old people are just full of advice," I said.

"There's tons of advice out in the world," Kurt said. "And it's each individual's choice about what advice to take."

"Good point, Kurt."

"Like coffee, we need filters," he said, taking a sip of his tall black coffee with no sugar. "Humans are hypocritical beings anyway," he added.

The ticket said we would be arriving in Berlin at 9:15 a.m. Not thinking clearly, I turned on my phone and checked the time. It was almost 8 a.m. Kurt asked me what my Berlin plan was and how he could help. I tried to lay it out for him: going to the Radisson (Kurt agreed to check in for me), the text to Alex to rendezvous in my room, the text to Victoria to come to my room, the moment of massive, epic humiliation and revenge...

KURT

"And then what?" I asked her.

"Well, Victoria will be devastated and Alex will have to choose me or her," Nia said, like an amateur.

"And what if he runs after her instead of you?"

"I don't think he will."

"But say he does," I said.

"Then at least I'll have ruined whatever they had between each other."

"And that will make you feel good? Satisfied?"

"Hey, I thought you were on my side. You promised," she said.

"I am and I did," I said. "I just want you to consider some things that your predecessor, the Count of Monte Cristo, did not think about."

"I know, I know," she repeated, "Going too far with vengeance."

"Not only that, but to consider its efficacy," I said. "Will it make you *feel better* the next day? Will you be any happier knowing that others suffered? And who knows how long their suffering, or your guilt, will last?"

"Guilt? Suffering? You're the one who's killed three people!" she jabbed.

I scanned the cafe car to make sure no one had heard Nia's damning comment.

"Nia, that's not fair," I said. "And I never planned on killing anyone."

"So it's my plan—my intention that makes this bad?" she said, clearly frustrated.

"I didn't say it was bad, you did. I simply asked you to consider some questions."

"Okay, Socrates, thanks for the inquiry approach," she quipped.

I took another sip of my coffee and pondered getting up and leaving the little smart aleck behind. But I had signed up for this. The girl needed help in more than one way. So, without worrying about her response, I spoke.

"Nia, I think you need to understand something: I am asking you these questions because—though I've only known you a short time—I care about you. I want you to be happy, to find true happiness. Now you're mocking me because what I said made you feel uncomfortable or less confident in your plan. This is usually when parents or adults walk away from teenagers and let them figure it out for themselves. Ultimately, you will have to find your own way, but I'm not going anywhere. You know why?— Because you're fourteen and you still need a helluva' lot of guidance."

"And you're eighty-nine and you're wanted for murder," she said. "What's in *your* coffee today, Kurt?"

"You asked me for help, and you know my Kung Fu skills are a bit rusty, so words are the only thing—"

"—So now we're joking?"

"Unless you want to listen to me," I made my condition clear.

"Okay, I promise I will listen to the very next thing you say," she declared. I put out my hand and she shook it, with a mocking smile on her face.

She was exasperating, yes, but also a kick in the pants.

A moment later, music blared from Nia's pocket. It was her phone ringing. She pulled it out, made a horrified face, and showed me the screen. It said "MOM" across the bottom. Nia's eyes glazed over with fear.

"Answer it," I said.

She shot me an incredulous glare.

"You promised to listen to the next thing I said," I reminded her.

NIA

I didn't want to talk to my mom. It was too risky. It might give away our location. But a promise was a promise, and I had just given the old man an ultimatum about hypocrisy. Before I answered Kurt told me to tell her the truth, to put her mind at ease, and not to worry: everything would still go on as planned. I hit the answer button and put it on speakerphone so Kurt could hear.

MOM: Hello! Oh my God. Nia, are you there?

ME: Hi Mom, it's me.

MOM: Oh my god! She picked up (this was said to someone next to her). Are you okay? Please tell me they didn't hurt you!

ME: Mom, I'm fine. Nobody hurt me. I haven't been kidnapped. I left on my own.

MOM: What?! I—I'm confused. Where are you?

ME: I can't tell you that. I can tell you tonight.

MOM: Nia, you listen to me. Are you alone?

ME: I'm with—I'm alone. I ran away. I didn't think you or Dad would even notice.

MOM: Nia, what are you talking about?! Please talk to me. Tell me the truth. Where are you? Your father and I are coming to get you immediately.

ME: I'm safe and fine and that's all I can tell you right now, mom. I ran away.

MOM: Nia, Goddammit do not play games with me! You have no idea how big this is. Where are you and who are you with?

ME: I'll call you tonight. Don't be mad at me, please.

MOM: Wait!

ME: Bye.

End call.

I turned off my phone, shoved it in my pocket, and looked at Kurt.

"How did I do?"

"Not bad," he said.

KURT

Now things were getting intense, even for a geezer like me. Nia and I went back to the cabin after our coffee and croissant breakfast. I was glad that she'd talked to her mom, but she didn't seem too happy about it. After we both had packed up our few things and were ready to arrive in Berlin with thirty minutes or so to spare, I broke the silence.

"I'm glad you talked to your mom," I said. "Now she won't be worried to death."

"Well, the only problem is that everyone knows where we are now."

"Do you think your phone's tracking thing-a-ma-jig works that well?" I asked. To me the technology sounded like something out of a James Bond movie, not reality.

"I really don't know, let's see," she said.

Nia went to tapping and swiping her little index finger across the screen of her phone. Her reading eyes, moving swiftly from left to right, went from curious to shocked.

"Oh, my God," she blurted. "It's traceable whether it's online or not! It's been traceable almost this whole time. They know exactly where we are!"

"I'll be damned," I said. "I guess we'll find out when we hit Berlin."

"Not if I can help it," Nia said. "It was stupid of me to not read the tracking device information earlier!"

Without a hint of hesitation, Nia opened the window slot and dropped her $400 phone from the train. We didn't even hear it hit the ground.

"That takes care of that," she said.

"Holy cow," I said.

I sat there without another word. I could have offered my thoughts on the matter, but Nia didn't appear to be in the right state of mind to receive them. So I pulled out my toiletry bag and a small water bottle, and began taking my morning medication.

"I hope ditching that thing works," Nia said, "Otherwise there's going to be lots of police and maybe even my parents waiting for us in Berlin."

"We'll hope for the best," I said.

"Do you ever worry about anything, Kurt?"

"I try not to."

With ten minutes to go until we arrived in Berlin, I figured it was the best time to impart some advice to young Nia. If the authorities were waiting at the station, it might be the last time I'd ever have a chance to talk to my rebellious temporary granddaughter. Plus, after speaking to her mom and throwing her phone out the window, she'd taken on an unpleasant air. However, feeling the enormous gap in our ages, I didn't know exactly where to start with her.

"You've missed two days of school," I said. "As a former teacher, I'm required to tell you that you should contact your teachers to see what work you've missed."

She threw me a saucy stare but said nothing.

"And don't ask them if you missed anything *important* while you were gone. Teachers hate that."

"Um, what's happened to you, Kurt?" she said. "You used to be cool."

"That one hurt, Nia," I said.

"Honestly, I never do homework, never study, and fail most of my tests just to piss off my parents."

"You think that's a good idea?" I said.

"Why not?"

"Well, it sounds like you're only hurting yourself."

"Oh, is that the moral of the story, grandpa?"

"No moral or morality behind it. It's just logic," I said. "Why deprive yourself of your education? Your education is yours, not your parents'. It's an age-old trap. In trying to punish someone else, you just end up punishing yourself."

"Where'd you get that one, gramps?

"I don't remember."

"Maybe you have a book of old man-isms that you forgot about."

Her attitude was turned up a few notches, perhaps at the mere thought of rethinking her view of her parents—or maybe it was the high probability of getting caught and the end of her adventure that was fast approaching. Regardless, I had to get my final word in.

"Now that I think of it, maybe this whole mission to stop the meeting between Alex and what's-her-name isn't about revenge or romance at all. Maybe it's all about your parents? You haven't had their attention for so long, you want to punish them by—

"Stop it!" she yelled.

"I'm just clari—

"What kind of a partner-in-crime are you if you keep questioning everything?"

"I didn't say anything about partners-in-crime," I said. "I agreed to *help* you."

"Okay, Socrates, is this why you're questioning me to death?

"Yes," I said.

"Are you finished?" Her voice cracked a bit, but she was too stubborn for tears.

"Almost," I said. "We've all lied, right? I've seen you lie and I've had eighty-some odd years experience with various forms of lying."

"Yes, humans do lie," Nia confirmed. "And?"

"And have you heard what the problem is with lying to *others*?"

"Something about how you're digging a hole for yourself to fall into one day?"

"Yes."

"Heard that one before," she mocked.

"Good," I said. "Do you know what the problem with lying to *yourself* is?"

"What?"

"That the hole you're digging is inside of you."

Nia turned her gaze out the window. It took her a few seconds to mold her expression into the stoic state she wanted. The train was slowing and the PA speakers alerted passengers in German and English that we would be arriving at Berlin *Hauptbahnhof* station in two minutes.

"What's the plan?" she asked, huffy yet business-like.

"Act natural," I said.

"You've gotta be kidding me."

NIA

Before our train came to a complete stop, I could see the railway platform crawling with armor-vested, machine-gun strapped military police officers. There were so many of them it almost made me faint. The scene also made my anger and annoyance with Kurt's grandpa advice quickly disappear. *Could they all be here for me and Kurt?* It didn't seem possible, but then again there was murder and kidnapping involved, and our story—as misreported as it was—was all over the news.

Kurt told me to stop staring out the window with my mouth agape. "Not very natural," he said. He advised that we walk slowly, keep our heads on straight, and be calm if spoken to. He reminded me that if we panicked, ran or resisted, things would get ugly and could be very dangerous.

"If we're caught, we're caught," he said, "Don't run."

I didn't want it to end, but I realized that Kurt was right. It looked like a police state out there. Kurt was correct about a lot of things, but I really didn't want my adventure to stop, my mission to fail. I had a plan to carry out.

I threw on my backpack and led us to the exit doors in between train cars. With each step I felt like this was it. *Game Over.*

Before we stepped off the train, Kurt gave me a nervous smile and signaled me to lock arms with him on his right side, opposite where he carried his cane.

I whispered to him, "The cane might look suspicious."

"Too late now," he said.

I expected to walk a few steps along the platform and be spotted, barked at in German, thrown to the ground and handcuffed. But we walked by the first two Robocops and nothing happened. I couldn't help but turn my head left and right, glancing at all the officers who looked dressed for a full-scale riot. For a few moments it was eerily quiet and uneventful until I saw four cops emerge from the crowd, running toward us. One of them yelled, *Halt!* I froze and Kurt jolted my arm as if to say, keep moving. But I couldn't. I braced myself for impact—the manhandling and the arrest.

When the four cops rushed right past us still yelling halt, I couldn't believe it. Strangely enough, I was almost disappointed that their attention was focused somewhere else. Me, Kurt, and everyone else in the area turned to witness as the four police officers grabbed three young bearded men and one woman wearing a hijab. I'd learned what a hijab was because I had read an American novel about a Muslim woman who had issues wearing the thing in Afghanistan. I didn't know for sure, but I guessed that the German police were onto these four people as possible terrorist suspects. I had no clue whether they were being unjustly profiled, or were simply refugees. I remained silent. I still couldn't believe that Kurt and I weren't the only fugitives on that train.

"Let's go," Kurt said.

He gently tugged on my wrist and I continued walking arm-in-arm with my fake grandpa.

It was kind of funny.

He'd told me to act natural and the old guy was sweating and panting like a dog.

KURT

From the moment we stepped off that train, I assumed we were goners. Hell, they might have even shot me down in cold blood. Who was I anyway? Just an old fart foreigner assumed to be a murderer, kidnapper, and who-knows-what-else!

When the armed policemen darted at us I damn near stuck my hands in the air in surrender, but I had to at least try to follow the advice I'd given Nia. When the Middle Eastern-looking refugees were apprehended, I couldn't believe it. Were they guilty of something? Or were they perfectly innocent humans that were being targeted because they were Muslim? Were they fleeing a war-torn country—or all of the above? After all, the world had become a strange, complicated place and it had all gotten away from me years ago.

Nia and I exchanged an expression of disbelief, turned away from the police scene, and walked up the stairs and into the main station. The glass ceiling structure seemed more like a new shopping mall than a European train station. Aside from Nia's little plan, getting out and seeing modern Berlin interested me since I'd never been there. I'd only seen old photographs of a decimated, shell-shocked city after the war.

Somewhere between disembarking from the train and getting into the main area of the *Hauptbahnhof*, I was hit by a wave of discomforting symptoms, but ignored them to the best of my ability. Body aches and pains had become an everyday thing for me. The usual suspects were my perennially sore feet, arthritic knees, aching hip, bad back and stiff neck. So when I felt hot flashes and was gripped by a sharp, aching pressure in my chest, I didn't become alarmed until Nia noticed that I was sweating profusely.

"Are you okay, Kurt?" she asked.

As those words left her mouth they sounded muted, like I was going deaf. I stopped moving my feet. Colors faded. I went down to one knee right there in the middle of the *Hauptbahnhof* and blacked out.

NIA

I wasn't certain that Kurt was having a heart attack, but I guessed so since he'd pressed one of his hands to his chest right before he passed out. When Kurt went down to one knee and then dropped unconscious, his head hit the floor. The blunt force split his skin and blood oozed on the ground. That's when I screamed.

A German man in a green maintenance uniform who must have worked at the station came to us and crouched down to help. He recognized that I was a foreigner and called an ambulance without asking many questions. It all happened so fast: Two paramedics came with a stretcher. They picked him up and I followed them to a van. We got in the back. Sirens blared. One guy spoke German mixed with English to ask me what happened. In shock, I couldn't say much. I told him he was my grandfather and that he collapsed without any warning. It was all too much. I sat in the back of the loud racing ambulance staring down at an unconscious Kurt.

How was this happening?
Was he going to die?
What was I going to do?
Was it all my fault?

Was my life and his crumbling to dust right in front of me?

My adventure had turned into a surreal nightmare. I didn't want Kurt to die—he couldn't die! But he hadn't opened his eyes or showed any signs of life since he collapsed. In what seemed like a minute, the vans' sirens went silent and we pulled up to the hospital. Kurt was whisked off to the emergency room. I trailed behind and was left in an endless, colorless hallway with two disturbing questions: Am I ever going to talk to Kurt again? And, why do all hospital hallways look and smell the same?

I stared at the clock in the waiting room. 10:41 a.m. How was I going to carry out my plan at the Radisson without Kurt? How could I get a hotel room? How was I going to deal with the consequences of all this? He was the calm one. He was the adult. Then I remembered that I didn't even have a cell phone anymore. *What was the plan now?!*

I had nothing.

For the first time in days, I felt like I was trapped, constantly checking the big, classroom-like clock on the wall.

11:15 a.m. The random German magazine pictures were not helping distract me. Was Kurt dead? And if he was dead, did any of my Alex-Victoria plan matter anymore? How could I be so selfish about this whole thing? Kurt's situation was life and death, my parents and the police were scouring Europe to find me, and I was worried about whether Alex liked me or not and how I could best make Victoria feel like a horrible slut. Perhaps this was the whole problem with *Monte Cristo* that Kurt was talking about. And maybe it was the major problem with the whole world. Selfishness.

11:32. Had they broken Anna? Did she squeal and give away everything? Would the police and my parents be waiting at the Radisson for me? If so, would some German cop have to wrestle me to the ground, or would I surrender peacefully?

I imagined myself doing some martial arts moves like Jason Bourne even though I'd never hit anyone in my life (nor had I studied any sort of martial art).

11:38. How would Alex respond to seeing me—with a loving smile or a scornful glare? I still couldn't figure out what had happened between us. How did it go from "love" to abandonment? There must have been one instant when everything changed for him. When was it? Was there any logic behind his actions, or was he just another thoughtless, impulsive, teenage boy? And then there was the most depressing idea of all: Maybe there was never anything real between me and Alex in the first place.

I should forget the Radisson plan altogether.

I would stay with Kurt.

At 11:45 a blonde-haired, tattooed nurse stood in front of me and told me that I could go in and say hello to my grandfather. She led me to a door and spoke to me as if I were five years old:

"Your grandfather had a heart attack. He might seem a bit weak and slow but his heart is working fine now."

I walked in alone and gasped at the site of Kurt in a hospital bed with tubes up his nose and stuck into his exposed, wrinkled arms. He had stitches above his right eye, which was black and blue. His eyes were closed. I whispered his name and he didn't respond. He looked dead.

Holding back tears, I started talking to him. I told him that he couldn't die today because I needed him to live. I needed a friend. I needed a grandfather. I needed the wisdom of someone who'd lived a long life, someone who had loved so genuinely. I apologized to him for being selfish and only thinking of myself and not being a good listener when he was giving me valuable advice. I bowed my head, closed my eyes and prayed, but I didn't have much practice at praying so I just ended up repeating: 'Please don't be dead, please don't be dead...'

While I was repeating my line and increasingly losing hope, Kurt said "I'm not dead" out loud and completely freaked me out! *I* almost had a heart attack from the pure shock of hearing his voice.

KURT

I faintly remember hearing Nia speaking to me. I could tell where I was from the smell alone—universal hospital odor. Nia was in the midst of some kind of confession and then she was pleading for me not to be dead when I said my first words out loud: "I'm not dead"—which sounds obvious and simple but was as philosophically important to me as "I think, therefore I am" was for Descartes.

Nia stared at me as if I were a ghost arisen from the grave. Her stunned expression amused me, but I couldn't laugh.

"Are you...okay?" she asked.

"Not bad, actually. They must have me on a helluva lot of pain killers."

"I was worried about you," she said.

"Thanks for caring," I croaked. "I'm sorry, but it looks like I won't be able to make it to the Radisson. The nurse said I would be kept here for twenty-four hours."

"Oh my God, Kurt, I don't want you to even think about my drama. It's stupid. I don't even think I'm gonna go anymore. I'll stay here with you."

There was a spark in her that had been missing that morning. She genuinely cared and seemed to have put

175

some consideration into her own pain. I was proud of her, which was possibly why I didn't want her story to end in that hospital room.

"Nia, do you think Alexander Dumas would think your plan is stupid?"

"Maybe. I don't know," she said, perhaps more receptive to my words than ever. Almost dying can have this effect, I guess.

"You know what would be stupid?" I said. "To ditch school, travel more than 1,500 kilometers, freak everyone out, make the news, and then not go down the final mile to do the thing you came here to do."

"But I don't think it's even worth it anymore."

"Think *what* is worth it?" I said. "You don't have to stick to your original plan, but you should confront the boy. See it through."

"What do I say to him?" Nia inquired.

"That's up to you," I said. "You're a clever girl. I'm sure you'll do fine."

Nia paused, gazed at my wrinkly old hand and nodded her head.

"Just promise to be alive when I get back," she said.

"I promise," I said. "Can you promise me something?"

"What?"

"Give your parents a chance."

"Do you mean give them *a call*?"

"No, I said 'a chance.'"

"Why?"

"Because parents aren't perfect," I said.

"But they're at least supposed to pay attention—to care about me," she said, "Seriously, they've both been ignoring me for years—even *before* the divorce."

I caught my breath. All the talking had made me light-headed. I was still feeling weak, but had to tell her something important before I faded out of consciousness again.

"Do you know the Parent Cycle, Nia?"

"The Parent Cycle?"

"When we are little kids—and, yes, even I was a kid once—we look up to our parents," I explained slowly. "We *worship* them because they are larger than life. They protect and feed us. They know everything and are infallible, like Gods. Then we hit the second phase, our teen years, and we see that our parents don't know everything, can be overprotective, incorrect and annoying, so we *blame* them for disappointing us and find new idols. That phase might last for decades, but eventually you get to the third phase: *Forgiveness*. As an adult you have your own kids and realize that life is difficult, parenting is hard, and that we all have our imperfections and issues."

"Why are you telling me all this?"

"Because the sooner you get to the forgiveness part, the better your life is going to be. Not only will you stop punishing your parents, but you'll stop punishing yourself in the process."

Nia seemed to quell the urge to come up with a punchy retort. Maybe she was past that now. She looked at my old wrinkly left hand again before gently taking hold of it.

"You might be the wisest man I know," Nia said.

"Thank you," I said.

"...Except for the murdering, kidnapping, runaway teenager's accomplice part."

"*Touche*," I said with a smile.

She took a step back to indicate she was leaving.

"Any final words of advice?" she asked. "And don't say, 'Act natural.'"

She peered at me expectantly—still just a kid.

"Whatever happens," I said, "learn from it."

NIA

I asked the plump receptionist at the hospital how far we were from the Radisson *Alexanderplatz*. She said, in surprisingly good English, that I could walk there. She pointed it out on a map and two minutes later I was walking down a busy street, across a river to the Brandenburg Gate, and then left onto *Unter den Linden*. Though I missed Kurt's company, I was able to move faster and my thoughts sped up as well. As I scanned the area and brainstormed a new plan on the fly, I imagined myself the new female version of Jason Bourne.

One big problem: I had no phone and needed one badly.

I popped into a Vodafone store and bought the cheapest cell phone available. The employee inserted a new SIM card and immediately activated my new toy. Because it was as cheap as a disposable, they didn't need any of my personal information. The only problem was that I had no internet connection. I walked out of the store and called one of the only numbers I had memorized: my best friend's. *Anna*. She picked up after the third try and was shocked to hear my voice.

"Holy shit, is this really you, Nia?"

"Yeah, but please chill for a second. I need your help."

"Where are you?" she asked.

"First I need to know: Did you tell anyone I was going to Berlin?"

"No..." Anna's pregnant pause frightened me. "But I did say I'd chatted with you in Budapest and that you weren't kidnapped but—

"Okay. That's fine," I said.

"Nia, do you realize—"

"Yes, I read the news."

"Everyone's looking for you!"

With that comment, imagining video cameras and agents all around me, I turned off the crowded *Unter den Linden*.

"Anna, can you log onto my profile and get Alex's number?"

"Yes," she said, "Anything for you."

"You're awesome."

I heard her fast typing on her laptop as I gave her my username and password.

"Are you sure you're OK?"

"Yeah, I'm good. I'm almost there."

"You're totes crazy, ya' know."

"Maybe a little," I said. "Do you have his number?

"Yep."

"I love you. Thank you!"

"I'm sending it now."

I thanked her again, hung up, and entered Alex's number without wasting any time. I stopped walking and leaned up against an old brick building that might have survived World War II. Hitting the call button, I inhaled deeply, hoping to produce the best British accent I had ever done.

Alex: Hello.

Me *(fake British)*: Hello, this is Margaret from the school event at the Radisson... We're conducting a survey of the student participants this evening and would like to know your room number, please.

Alex: Um, Margaret from...?

Me: Yes, with the ISS center. We contract with the Radisson as well as the Wesley Prep School... and its subsidiaries.

Alex: Oh, okay. My room is 614... Do you need anything else?

Me: Um, just your planned arrival time for the next conference session.

Alex: Uh, 4pm. All sessions start at that time.

Me: Excellent. Tally-ho!

I hung up and, aside from saying "tally ho"—don't know where that one came from—I was pretty proud of myself and my new, crappy phone. It was 1:45. I had enough time to catch him. I walked back to *Unter den Linden* and revised my plan in stride. It was a lively, beautiful street with a mixture of very old and quite new architecture. Something about being on my own in a big city put a hop in my step. My walk turned into a jog and then a run—for no reason at all. Maybe the adrenaline and my sense of purpose gave me extra fuel. It was exhilarating. When I made it to the big square, I stopped to catch my breath.

I picked up a coffee to go in the middle of Alexanderplatz square, noticed the Radisson hotel sign in the distance, and took a moment to gather myself. I gazed up at the Soviet-style space-needle TV tower. Dizzied by its height, I asked myself: What would Monte Cristo do? What would Katniss do? What would Kurt do? And it hit me that I was asking the wrong questions.

What would Nia do? I was the main actor in this movie—a unique Bulgarian-American hybrid—and so I would have to write my own script.

The lobby of the Radisson was what you might expect of a downtown hotel in Berlin: a post-Communist 1990s vision of futuristic chic—a touch classier than IKEA. A few high school students with lanyards around their necks were milling around, staring into their cell phone screens. Nobody seemed to notice me. I approached the front desk lady and asked to be connected to my colleague, Alex, in room 614.

"Your colleague?" she asked.

"I want to make sure he's ready for the next conference session," I told her.

"Of course," she said.

The receptionist picked up the phone and was soon greeting Alex on the other end. When she handed me the phone, I almost lost my cool and ran away, but grabbed it before it got awkward. I went full British again.

Alex: "Hello?"

Me: "Hello, this is Margaret again."

Alex: "Ummm, okay..."

Me: "I just want to say thank you very much for participating in our survey."

Alex: "Um, I'm not sure—"

Me: "Good day, sir."

I handed the receptionist the phone and she gave me a curious stare as I speed-walked away with my coffee still in hand. She must have thought it was some kind of teen prank. I went around the corner to the elevator and scrunched inside the crowded, stainless steel box before the doors slid shut. I hit the button for the sixth floor but it didn't light up like the others. I tried again and a pasty, middle-aged woman in a business suit told me that I needed a key card. Every little setback I now saw as a challenge to overcome. *If I made it this far, anything is possible.*

"Yeah," I said, "That's why I have to go back to my grandfather's room, because I forgot my key."

A random guy held out his key card and told me to hit the sixth floor button again. *Grandpa Kurt was helping me and he didn't even know it!*

I stepped onto the sixth floor and strategically dropped my coffee lid in a small ashtray-topped trashcan. I hurried to room 614 and tried not to worry about much. Only two words were on repeat in my head: *Coffee. Spill. Coffee. Spill.* I knocked, Alex opened the door, and it took a moment for my presence to sink in. His jaw slowly dropped. He'd mastered the dumb-boy-expression.

"Nia, what the hell are you doing in Berlin?"

"Um, emergency," I said. "My grandfather had a heart attack."

Alex looked very confused.

"Aren't you happy to see me?" I asked.

"I—this is crazy. I just heard you were kidnapped by some murderer!"

"Well, it's a long story. Can I come in?" I asked, while walking in.

While Alex was disarmed, I went to hug him—planning on splashing coffee on the back of his shirt—but he did a quick sidestep, put up his hand in defense, and I ended up spilling the lukewarm coffee all over the front of my own shirt.

"Ahhh!" I yelled.

"Oh crap," Alex said. "I'm sorry."

Channel Kurt. Act natural. Don't worry.

"I'm the one who's sorry, Alex." I said politely. "Can I use your bathroom?'

"Sure."

He was clearly freaked out. I closed the bathroom door and immediately saw his phone on the counter. *Bingo.* I picked it up and it was unlocked. In that moment, I had no problem altering my crappy plan and invading his privacy. His text messages were flooded by one name—Victoria. I hit reply and sent her a message from his phone: *"Come to my room right now. It's an emergency."* I put his phone back on the counter. I opened the bathroom door, strolled into the bedroom, and semi-posed with my hand on my hip in front of the TV. Alex was sitting on the bed, still in disbelief.

"Why did you come here, Nia?" he asked, nervously.

"Well..."

I had planned my strategy but I hadn't planned on explaining myself.

"Are you in danger? Is the murderer guy like outside and—"

"No, I'm fine." I said. "Why did you stop sending me messages?"

He said nothing for a few seconds, then offered a pathetic: "I don't know."

"'I don't know.' That's it?" I asked.

Selfish. All of us are selfish.

"It's complicated," he said, as if he had chosen one out of three lame multiple-choice answers in his head.

"I'm sure it is," I said sarcastically, then pointed to my stained T-shirt. "Hey, do you have a shirt or something I could change into? I'll take anything that isn't coffee-stained."

"Yeah."

He grabbed a T-shirt, one of the ones they gave out free at the conference, and lobbed it to me from a few feet away. I understood I'd surprised him and we were officially broken up, but he'd been noticeably cold to me. No hug, no kiss on the cheek, no pat on the shoulder. Nothing.

It hurt.

"Aren't you too young to be drinking coffee?" he said.

I laughed, almost maniacally.

"Aren't you too young to be two-timing?" I said.

"Wait, what the hell's going on here?" he said, looking really pissed.

"Why did you text me referring to our song, 'Nothing Compares to You'?"

Again, he had no answer, just a dumb-boy-expression.

That text must have been one of many forgotten flirty messages he'd sent to girls to get nothing more than an ego-boosting response.

"Well, here's my response," I told him.

That's when, perfectly on cue, Victoria knocked on the door. Alex gave me a suspicious glare and I gave him a knowing smirk. As Alex went to the door, his back to me, I stripped off my stained shirt and stood there topless, wearing only a black bra. I watched as Alex kept the door mostly closed, sticking his head out into the hall to talk to Victoria. I yelled "Hi Victoria!" and that was it. He opened the door in defeat and Victoria strolled in with total disgust and anger on her face.

"What the hell?" she shouted, looking me up and down for a second.

Victoria turned away and gave Alex a death stare. "Well? Are you gonna answer me, *mrasnik!*"

Mrasnik is a Bulgarian word that roughly translates to "lying, cheating bastard." It was music to my ears. Alex cowered but said nothing.

"What is *she* doing here?" Victoria said, "Are you deaf now?"

I remained standing in front of the widescreen television and, along with Victoria, waited for Alex's response.

"I don't know," he muttered.

I had never seen Alex so weak and pathetic. It felt good, but not quite good enough.

"He invited me," I lied.

Victoria turned her attention back to me.

"And *who* are you, again?" she said. "Oh, wait. Are you little Nia from the international school in Sofia?"

"Little?" I said.

"Robbing the cradle now, Alex?"

Alex puffed up his chest as if he needed to be inflated to speak up.

"She's lying," he said and pointed at me. "I never invited Nia here."

Both sets of eyes were on me again.

"Lying?" I said, "Were you lying when you said you loved me in the middle of August?"

Alex froze. He didn't see that one coming. The mention of August was salt on his increasingly exposed wounds.

"August?" Victoria said, with a sharpness I could feel. "Tell me you didn't."

"It's not what you think," Alex told her.

"No, so far it's much worse," she said.

I expected Victoria to turn to me and explode, to call me a little bitch—maybe even attack me. Instead, she leapt at Alex and started hitting him with balled fists. He put his hands up to ease the blows, but he didn't fight back. Maybe he knew he deserved it.

After thirty seconds of throwing roundhouses, Victoria sat down at the edge of the plush bed, hid her head in her hands, cursed between her heavy breaths, and cried. Alex alternated between inarticulately trying to explain the situation to her and shooting me glassy, betrayed eyes. Monte Cristo was right, forget blood—revenge was more painfully dished out with emotional and psychological stabs. Having gotten the desired effect and feeling uncomfortably naked, I pulled on the conference T-shirt. Clothed again, I did something entirely unexpected.

I cried too.

"Why are *you* crying?" Victoria asked.

I was too busy bawling to answer her right away. It took me awhile to calm myself enough to speak. I was also stalling because I had no idea what to say. All I knew was that the emotions I expected to have were entirely different from the ones I was having. When I recovered enough to talk, they listened.

"I'm crying because I truly feel bad for what I've done," I said. "I feel sorry for us, Victoria. We are smart, educated, independent girls—and look what we've let happen to us. We liked the same boy so you posted cute, cuddly pictures with him online, and I sent him flirty texts. We wanted to hurt each other. When I felt neglected and jealous I wanted to get back at *you*—not him. I wanted Alex's love and attention but was totally blind to all the signs of my neediness, insecurity, and selfishness; without seeing that he didn't love, adore or even truly care for me."

Their attention was rapt. The words coming out of my mouth surprised us all.

"I never questioned myself and my motives. I just wanted to reverse what I called 'The Epic Devastation.' I wanted you both to feel bad, and now that I have, it's horrible. It's pointless."

"—I mean, Alex should feel bad," I continued, pointing at him. "You should be the one crying, and you're the only one who isn't! Love is not a word you can throw around, and girls do not exist for you to bounce between because it makes you feel good about yourself—makes you feel loved. I thought I loved you, but now that seems like a ridiculous joke."

I turned my attention toward Victoria.

"And you have to decide if you want a guy like Alex, or if you want someone who will truly give himself to you and sacrifice for you. For me, I see that Alex is far from being that kind of person, and it's not my job to try and make him—or any boy—like me, pay attention to me, or protect me."

The two of them just sat there on the edge of the bed, staring at me like I was from an alien planet.

There were three loud knocks at the door that startled all of us.

"Polizei, offen."

It was the police, I understood that much—but I wasn't finished yet.

I moved over to position myself between Victoria, Alex, and the door.

"Nia, we need to open the door," Alex said.

I ignored him and kept talking.

"It took me awhile to get here. I haven't slept much or even taken a shower in three days, but I don't care. I thought I was coming to Berlin because of you two, but it was really for me—for *this*. I realize that I'm young and have a lot to experience in life, but at least I know something now that I didn't before: The most important things in life are trust, kindness, and finding real love—real relationships—

"Polizei, öffne die Tür!"

"I'm sorry for bothering you two, but I really hope you think about what I said—especially you, Victoria, because we don't need to put up with this. Alex is the one who needs to figure his shit out. You might think I sound crazy but I've been listening to a wise old man lately—a man who almost died today. *That* is important, *that* is something worth worrying about, worth fighting for. All this other stuff just seems like a game we play, and I'm done playing."

I crossed my arms defiantly.

"Game Over."

"Open the door!" the policeman shouted in English this time.

Alex and Victoria were both silent. Like *catatonic*. They must have thought I was either wise beyond my years or completely insane—or both. I grabbed my stained shirt and walked to the door.

"I'm opening the door," I said. "Please don't hurt me."

"Come out with your hands on the top of your head," he said.

I opened the door and four uniformed German cops flooded in with their guns drawn.

They verified that I was Nia Mladenova and handcuffed me. Strangely, as we left the room and descended in the elevator, I felt pretty damn good about myself. That is, until I was greeted in the downstairs lobby by at least ten more police officers, cameras, reporters, and blaring sirens.

This was serious.

KURT

It was dusk outside when I woke up in the Berlin hospital. Nia was by my side. There were two police officers standing in the open doorway watching me. Nia had a grave expression that told me her adventure had come to an end.

"Are you okay?" she asked.

"I don't feel any younger, but I'm fine."

"You called them, didn't you?"

"Your parents? Yes," I said, "After you left the hospital, I waited about an hour to let you do what you had to do."

"Thank you," she said.

She didn't seem upset. She appeared oddly at ease and more adult, as if she'd adopted a new layer of maturity since I'd last seen her.

"Are your parents here yet?"

"They're on their way," Nia said. "But there are about six police officers and a detective outside."

"Holy cow, should I be scared?"

"I don't know," she said. "They said I can only talk to you for a minute."

"How'd it go with what's-his-name?" I asked.

"Not as planned," Nia said with a smirk.

I only smiled because a chuckle would have hurt. "There's a saying: If you want to make God laugh, tell him about your plans."

"Is that another one of your original grandpa-isms?" she asked.

"That one's a Woody Allen rip off," I said. "So did you feel like The Count of Monte Cristo?"

"There were some moments," she said. "But the Count didn't wear a bra."

"I'm not gonna ask," I said and paused. "Did you learn anything?"

Nia grinned. "Tons."

Then she told me about her wonderful speech.

NIA

After I talked to Kurt, they left two officers at his hospital door to make sure the old guy wouldn't escape, and shuffled me off to the police station. One policeman told me that they'd slapped Kurt with a long list of criminal charges that were absolutely ludicrous, but they were taking it all very seriously. I waited alone for about an hour in a holding area that felt more like a doctor's waiting room than a prison cell.

At any minute I expected Coriolanus Snow to come in and interrogate me. So when the door finally opened and my parents came in, all flustered—looking like they hadn't slept in days, yet happy to see me—I was surprised. They both hugged me with tears in their eyes.

"*Dobre li see?*" my dad asked in Bulgarian. "Are you alright?"

"Are you hurt?" my mom said.

"What has happened?" my dad said, oddly, in English.

"We were worried sick about you!"

I gave them the very short version of my two days on the run, and apologized for everything—for leaving, stealing money, lying, misleading them, and not calling sooner.

Instead of yelling at me, deriding my behavior, and threatening me, they actually apologized to me!

"No, Nia," my mom said, "We're the ones who are sorry."

I was speechless.

"We..." my mom said and gazed at my dad like she actually respected him. "We talked quite a bit over the past two days and realized that we've become very bad parents."

My dad nodded, shamefaced.

"Even if your father and I don't get along, if our marriage is over, it shouldn't mean that we stop being parents," she said, tearing up, much more open than I'd ever witnessed. "I'm sorry we've been so selfish, Nia. I'm so sorry."

My dad nodded again.

"We make a nightmare of never seeing you again," my dad added, trying his best in English, but coming up short. Still, I understood exactly what he meant.

I was stunned, overwhelmed by emotion.

"I hope you understand that the divorce was necessary for us, Nia," my mom said, "But we both want a second chance at being good parents to you."

My dad nodded, saw that I was at a loss for words, and gave me a big hug.

I embraced both of them, cried, and said, "Me, too."

They understood what I meant: I wanted to be a better daughter, too.

It might sound cheesy, but it was genuine. I felt truly lucky for the first time in my life. I guess sometimes it takes crazy traumatic experiences to bring out the best in people—to make us appreciate what we have.

The reunion love fest didn't last long. My parents and I were separated, and I spent all that night alone in the interrogation room with Detective Schenck, who I referred to as the Detective Guy. He didn't talk to me like those aggressive jerk cops in American movies. Detective Guy reminded me more of a dorky middle school counselor. Still, he was serious and that made the atmosphere uneasy. I asked about Kurt's status and he wouldn't answer a single question about him except that he was alive and still in the hospital recovery room. Detective Guy wanted me to tell the whole story—stick to the facts only—and that was it. No more questions.

So I did.

His inquiry seemed never ending and kind of blurred together by the end, but I do remember this part clearly:

DETECTIVE GUY: Did you have any idea where you dropped your iPhone, Nia?

ME: No. I only remember it was not too far from Berlin.

DETECTIVE GUY: Schonefeld. Very close to Schonefeld airport.

ME: Ummm, why does that matter?

DETECTIVE GUY: It matters because we were having trouble tracking it on a moving train, but when it stopped moving we pinpointed the exact location. An entire tactical police unit was immediately dispatched to Schonefeld Airport at approximately 8:50 a.m. Saturday morning. Your parents were notified in Budapest, where we first thought you might be, based on your diversionary note. You had quite an expensive, tax-payer-funded reception waiting for you in Budapest *and* at Schonefeld airport, but you never showed up. We thought you two might be trying to catch a flight out of Europe.

ME: I really apologize, Detective. I told my mom I was all right on the phone. I told her I wasn't kidnapped and not to worry.

DETECTIVE GUY: I know. I was listening to that call.

That part was really like a movie because I found out just how many people were after me and Kurt, and that I was not only being tracked but was also under surveillance!

The next morning I sat in a small room with a German judge, the Detective Guy, a lawyer, my parents, and their lawyer. It was a kind of secret mediation that my parents insisted on to keep my story out of the media any further. They talked for almost two hours, using a lot of legal-speak that I didn't really understand. I made it a point to take the blame for my part in the whole thing—including convincing Kurt to stay with me, lying in the note, and not contacting my parents—and I defended Kurt for saving me, protecting me, and giving me good advice. At the end the judge and the lawyers said that if Kurt's story and mine matched up, then there was a slight chance he would be acquitted of the most serious charges. After re-assuring me, they dismissed my parents and I from the room to come up with their official decision.

They released me that afternoon. My parents and I hugged each other outside of the police building and we took a taxi straight to the airport. I asked about Kurt and they told me he would be in custody for another day or two, questioned, then released. Instead of being happy about the news of his probable release, my heart sank.

I might never see Kurt again.

KURT

The following evening, two kind police officers transported me from the hospital to a police station. They didn't bother to handcuff me, but did politely escort me to a barren, monochrome interrogation room with one table and two chairs. The guard motioned me to sit down across from a middle-aged man in a form-fitting dark suit.

"Hello, I'm Detective Schenck," he said with a subtle German accent.

"Kurt Chavez," I said. I would have added "Nice to meet you," but it didn't seem the time or place.

"Odd," he said, "Your first name is German and your last name is Spanish."

"Mexican, not Spanish," I said. "I'm half Mexican."

It wasn't the first time I'd had to make the distinction. By the intonation, some people seemed to think that calling me Spanish was a compliment, and Mexican was not.

"If you insist," he said. "Are you German too?"

"Yes, but it's a mix of German, English, and Dutch on my mom's side," I said. "In America we just call that 'white.'"

"Really?"

"Yes," I said. "I'm half white."

"Seems a strange category," the detective noted.

"Indeed."

"Can you confirm your age, Mr Chavez, for the record?"

"I'm a spritely eighty-nine."

The impressed yet bewildered expression on the detective's face was priceless.

"I have to admit," he said. "You two are quite the unusual suspects."

"I suppose so."

"I'm surprised this little fiasco didn't kill you, Mr Chavez."

"It almost did!"

"Mr Chavez, let's get to the facts of this case—which by the way—implicate you in many serious crimes. Are you aware of this?"

"Nia told me some of the news on the internets," I said. "And I can tell you right now, this kidnapping business is a bunch of malarkey."

"I don't know what 'malarkey' is, Mr Chavez," he said.

"But you can guess, right?"

"Please, begin with the moment you met Nia Mladenova."

"Well, for God's sake, this is gonna take a while..."

4 HOURS LATER...

201

Though I faced trumped up charges and an uncertain fate, I actually enjoyed telling the detective my story—our story—because it meant something dear to me.

And, no matter what happened, nobody could take that away.

"That just about covers it, Detective," I said. "I assume you've heard Nia's side of the story—maybe in this very room."

"Yes, Mr. Chavez. I appreciated your *very* detailed account," he said. "Are you finished?"

"Yes, sir."

"Your story concurs almost perfectly with Nia's."

"Almost?"

"Nia told us that—in the hospital—after..." The detective flipped through his notes and located the part he was searching for. "...She told you that she learned "tons" from the whole experience and explained her growth on the matter, she held your hand... and then said 'I love you.'"

The detective turned all his attention toward me.

"Um..." I hesitated. "That's correct."

"And how did you respond?"

"If you must know, Detective, I didn't say a word."

"Why?" he asked.

"Because I cried," I said.

"Because she saved your life?"

"For starters."

"I see," he conceded.

"Can I go home now?" I said.

"Not yet."

That night, I was fed a reasonable meal and slept in a moderately comfortable jail cell. The next morning I was escorted to my second and final meeting with Detective Schenck. He had two coffees in hand and offered me one.

"Thank you for your cooperation, Mr Chavez," he said. "Thanks to Nia's testimony and her parents' generous insistence, you can leave today—but under some strict conditions."

Detective Schenck slid a thick stack of papers across the table where I sat. It was dense enough to be a transcript of the Bible.

"Do I have to read all of this for Christ's sake?"

"No," he said, then pointed to the top of page one. "This is the summary. The result of the mediation is that all criminal charges against you have been dropped. The most important conditions are these: You must pay a fine to the German state of 2,350 euros for your medical expenses and costly inconvenience to the police department."

I groaned at first sight of the bill, but it made perfect sense. I was getting off easy.

"Fair enough," I said.

"You will be escorted to the airport tonight and must fly out of Germany, not to return for a period of ten years..."

"Fair enough."

Germany was overrated anyway.

"And you are not to, *under any circumstances*, resume communication with Nia Mladenova. In fact, there is an official restraining order. You are never to be found within 100 meters of Nia in the Eurozone," he asserted. "Do you understand?"

"I suppose so."

"Please sign here, Kurt."

I hesitated for a few moments. The legal agreement was all very rational, the opposite of my previous three days— three life-saving, unforgettable days. I would miss Nia dearly.

Though it pained me, I signed the document.

attn: Nia Mladenova
American International School,
13 Rakovski St, Sofia, Bulgaria 1000

Dear Nia,

I hope this letter finds you well and does not get either of us into any trouble. I'm sending it to your school because it's the only reference I have for you. As you know, this old fart doesn't use the internets and doesn't plan to.

Months ago, when we last spoke in that German hospital room, you kindly told me what you learned from me. Thank you for that. I am eternally grateful. Your sentiments moved me in such a way that I was speechless, overwhelmed. Choked up, I couldn't manage to say "I love you," but I do love you, Nia—like the grandfather you never had and like an old friend who cares deeply for you.

In the whirlwind of our journey and the selectiveness of our memory, perhaps you didn't realize what I learned from you. In short, I learned to appreciate the gift that is life—to want to be alive! If the detective did not tell you, I planned to commit suicide in my Budapest hotel room, so I could be done with this world and join my beloved Maria. But you were waiting there in my room, like an angel sent to save me. You lifted me out of despair, out of my pain and sense of purposelessness, with your call to adventure—your Monte Cristo-inspired mission. I think the world needs more of the romanticism of Dumas, more of the spirit, conviction, and courage that you have, Nia. For this I am eternally grateful, and I am optimistic about your future.

As for me, I'm ready to live my final days to the fullest. You have given me a new sense of purpose by inspiring me to write again. It might be my last book, but it could very well be my best—based on the adventure of a certain teenage girl I had the pleasure of meeting on the way to Budapest. However, I won't be able to do this story justice without your voice, so I need to ask you a big favor, Nia: Write. Write down your story from the day you left Sofia and met me. Write about Belgrade, Budapest, Berlin— everything. Write it and send it to me as soon as possible. I'll do my best to polish it up and include it in the final manuscript!

And if our book makes any money (no guarantees here), you can expect a royalty check in the mail. The rest of the profit will pay for my inanimate return to a special reserved plot in downtown Budapest. (*I still can't resist the morbid jokes!*)

Until then, I have a novel to finish.

Thank you,

Your dear friend,

-Kurt Chavez

Dominic Carrillo is a writer and teacher from San Diego, California. This is his fourth book. He's the author of *To Be Frank Diego*, *Americano Abroad*, and his award winning, debut YA novel *The Improbable Rise of Paco Jones*. Dominic lives in Sofia, Bulgaria. For more information check out his website: **www.dominicvcarrillo.com**

Carrillo's award-winning debut YA novel:

"All readers should find plenty here to make them smile. A fun, amusing tale about the beautiful torment of young hearts and hormones at play."
-*Kirkus Reviews*

"In the spirit of S.E. Hinton's *The Outsiders* and John Green's *Looking for Alaska*... A quick yet heavy-laden read about race, class, and friendship."
-*School Library Journal*

"Carrillo is an honest storyteller. He is able to illuminate his characters so that a greater truth about humanity comes shining through."
-*Underground Book Reviews*

SPECIAL THANKS

Writing, editing, and distributing a book is no small task. In addition to those who helped with the writing process, there are those who have sponsored and supported this book in many other ways. Their support has helped get this into the hands of more young readers, including donations to schools and libraries both in the USA and internationally. Thank you to the librarians, principals, teachers, colleagues and students around the world. My special thanks and love to Terry, Carolyn, Alida, Mary, Romi and Mama Jean.